Filled with heartfelt experiences, humorous, and definitely a unique way to look at life's miseries, ups and downs author Kenneth Weene has written another five star winner.

-Fran Lewis, author, book reviewer, and radio personality

Tales From the Dew Drop Inne
Kenneth Weene

ALL THINGS
THAT MATTER
PRESS

ISBN 13: 978-09847215-8-0
Library of Congress Control Number: 2012930636

Cover Art By: Maggie Evans
Cover design by All Things That Matter Press
Published in 2012 by All Things That Matter Press

CHAPTER 1 - HOME

Ephraim, my neighbor, wasn't much of a musician. But he could pick at a guitar and his voice didn't stray too far off track. That made him good enough for a part-time gig at the Dew Drop Inne. That's where he and I hung out.

There must be one of those pun-named bars in every town. Some have the extra "e" to make them sound classy and some don't. Other than that, they're all pretty much the same—dumps.

This one, it belonged to Sal Margioni, had an Irish theme courtesy of some four-leaf-clover decals and a sign for Killian's Red, which Sal didn't actually serve. He did make a bad Irish coffee using tar-like liquid from a seldom cleaned and long over-boiled pot topped with RediWhip.

Sal's own Irish roots could be traced back to Napoli on his father's side. His mother he described as a Heinz 57 American with a little Oneonta. Nobody ever told him that was a city; most of the customers at the Dew Drop wouldn't have known the difference; the rest of us just kept it as a joke. Occasionally, somebody would bring in a box of Oneida Biscuits, and we'd all smile—being sure to offer Sal one.

"Yous guys really like these things," he'd comment. "Me, I prefer a pretzel with my beer."

Actually, I never saw him eat a pretzel, but we all saw him drink that beer—glass after endless glass of Miller tap. Sal's gut had reached a size that was beginning to hamper him behind the beat-up bar. Some days he had to strain just to reach the handles to draw those glasses. His stained white shirts and checkered suspenders seemed to stress with the effort of keeping his body contained.

Sal was neither jovial nor talkative. "Enjoys yourself; Yous got money?; Yous want a drink?" were his mantras. Beyond that, he avoided words.

"Talkin' can get yous in trouble," Sal had answered when Tony asked him why he didn't talk with us, his regular customers. He followed that explanation with, "Yous want a drink?"

Ephraim's singing was certainly not the center of enjoyment or attraction. It wasn't much of a source of income, either. Sal didn't pay him but did allow Ephraim to put a tip jar on the table. We, mostly to fit in, would drop change in the jar. A drink, that was a shot of the cheap stuff and a small glass of draught, was a buck sixty. Ephraim got a lot of forty-cent tips that added up to his own hard-hitting consumption of rye and Budweiser.

If there was a center point to The Dew Drop, it was the pool table, one of those coin-operated deals that always seem to come with warped cues and uncooperative balls. Most of them also come with a local hustler. At the Dew Drop it was Jonny Scott. Jonny was easily the champion of the bar; most of us didn't bother to play with him, not even for fun. So he had to wait for new marks who'd drift in thinking they could play. In neighborhood joints like the Dew Drop, there aren't many drifters, so Jonny's pickings were pretty slim. He would have done better if he once in a while blew a game to one of us. Then we might have occasionally taken him on, especially after we had a few under our belts. But the guy couldn't ease off. It killed him to miss even one shot; that was unless he was hustling one of those marks.

At times it was suggested he try hustling somewhere else, somewhere where there might actually be a few guys who could play; but Jonny wasn't going anyplace. He was, like the rest of us, a regular. Once you've found a home, you don't leave it easily, especially when that home is the only one your mind can wrap around.

Most of us regulars had come from someplace, some other home. I guess that's true of everybody—we all come from somewhere. The thing about the people who make a neighborhood bar their home is that they don't want to acknowledge that somewhere. It's like we've been cast adrift on the ocean and come to rest on an island—not some lovely deserted oasis with palm trees and dancing girls—something more like an island of floating debris.

My own journey? I will admit that once I had a family, but I don't much talk about them. No, they aren't dead. I am. At least it seems.

My accent? You decide. Wherever you say, I'll own it. Like I said, there's a Dew Drop in every town so what does it matter?

Ephraim, on the other hand, he had a story, and he was willing to tell it. One afternoon, before we headed out for the Dew Drop, he shared it with me.

Not surprisingly, it started with his name. That tells you right off that he was from some kind of Bible sect. In his case, the Amish, right out of Pennsylvania.

Ephraim was the younger of two sons; the older was Emanuel. Their father's name was Joseph. Ephraim was the obvious name, just like it was all from the good book.

It was an embarrassment to his father, that he only had the two boys. "A good man should be blessed with many sons," he had told Ephraim and his brother many times.

It was also an embarrassment—a much greater one—when Joseph's wife, Asena, gave up on the marriage and the faith and went off with a Mennonite to open a pie shop in Des Moines. Why Des Moines? Ephraim didn't have an answer.

He had visited her once on his own journey, but Asena had told him nothing beyond a simple statement that she was happy, happy with her new husband Joshua, and happy with her faith, which was now Lutheran. She was not so happy with their daughter, but that was not his story to tell.

After Asena left, Joseph became bitter, not that he sounded all that sweet from the get go. The two boys were worked hard. Worse, they were constantly criticized and ridiculed. Emanuel, the older boy, courted their father's approval, married young, and settled down to a life of farming, crafts, and prayer.

Ephraim, who perhaps was more like his mother, left home at sixteen.

There's a popular belief that Amish teens go through a rite of passage, something called Rumspringa, when they go off and try the normal world. For most Amish that's just not true. It certainly wasn't for Joseph, who, when told of Ephraim's intent, declared his son dead. That was an end and shut of it.

At some point Ephraim had sent his brother a letter. It was returned with, "You are dead to us!" printed in large block across the page. There was no way to tell whose hand had done the writing, but the message was clear. I know this because Ephraim had kept that letter. It was pinned to the wall of his room, his only decoration.

"Why Albuquerque?" I asked him as we sat in his room.

"Why Des Moines?" He laughed wryly. "Once you drift, you drift. Where you land, you land."

"Would you go back? I mean if your father…"

"If Joseph would permit?"

"Okay, yeah. If Joseph would permit."

"To what?"

"To your home. To where you belong."

"You don't think I belong here?"

"As much as any of us."

"Right, as much as any of us."

We went to the Dew Drop to seal the conversation with a beer. One draught led to another. Ephraim picked up his guitar and started to strum. Another of the other regulars got the tip jar from behind the bar and set it next to him. Dropped in a quarter, a dime and a nickel.

Sal called out, "Enjoys yourself," and drew himself another glass.

Jonny asked, "Anybody want to shoot a game?" There were no takers.

Before he started to sing, Ephraim whispered to me, "See, I'm home."

"Yeah." I lifted my glass.

CHAPTER 2 - ANGELICA AT THE DEW DROP INNE

Angelica showed up about eight looking like a fifty-dollar whore and shaking her booty like a blender in heat. She was enough of a distraction that Jonny missed a shot, which bit him in the ass when Tom actually won the game, something that didn't happen often.

Even Ephraim, who isn't easily distracted, stopped strumming and singing.

I was nursing my Killer's Delight. It was a drink Sal had created weeks before because he'd watched Oliver Twist and bought too much gin. "Yous guys like gin," he'd announced, not asked.

Since most of the guys weren't buying it, Sal had decided it was my favorite and always had a killer on the bar before I could tell him otherwise.

This girl we'd never seen, this Angelica, came in and started making moves. Sal was first because she wanted a drink. "Hi, sweetie," she crooned and leaned over the bar to kiss him. It wasn't a friendly kiss—the kind a girl pecks on your cheek. Or even one of those firm lip kisses that say there might be something coming. It's a tongue in as far as it can go kind of kiss and leaves Sal red and wordless.

"Vodka," she demanded, "with a beer." Her voice was low and sultry and her wink suggestive.

Sal bobbed his head and reached for a bottle.

Before the shot and brew were on the bar, she'd moved on to Tom. I watched with awe and arousal. I've never seen another woman like her; I wasn't sure that I wanted to. Her hands were all over him. She found his sack and squeezed. Tony jumped and grimaced but couldn't say anything – her tongue was down his throat.

How long could that tongue be? Part of me wanted to find out; another part wanted to get out of there. Sometimes instincts just keep warning you.

Between drinks—many drinks, Angelica made her way around the room—tonguing and groping each of us until everyone had the kind of hard-on you get in junior high school; the kind that feels powerful and embarrassing at once.

"Who wants to take me home?" It was defiant, a schoolyard dare.

"What'll it cost?" Tom asked. I don't think anyone else would have had the cajones; Tom didn't give a damn, not about anything.

"Baby, when we're done, you tell me."

The smile on Angelica's face screamed *beware*. The grin on Tom's said this is gonna be something. The rest of us shuffled around and looked uneasy, embarrassed, and envious.

Angelica grabbed Tom's hand and with a swish of her ass led him out the door. They were gone before Sal could say, "What about your drinks?"

"Damn, who's gonna pay her tab?" Sal mumbled as he cleared away her empties.

That wasn't the last question. For weeks we wondered what had happened to Tom. He was gone, disappeared; nobody takes it lightly when a member of the family disappears.

We wondered until Jonny ran into him at O'Grady's. That's where the city's serious pool sharks hung and where the wanna-be's went to learn. "There he was," Jonny told us. "Tom sees me and looks like he wants to slide under that table. I walk over and hold out my hand. 'How you doing?' I ask. Tom just kind of gulps. Anyway, I got a game with Jack Morgan – you know him, right?"

Actually none of us knew Morgan, but we'd heard of the best player in town.

"I'm watching Jack run the table on me when Tom comes over. 'You know, Jonny, that dame I took off with.' I just nod. 'Well, she weren't no dame at all. Who'd have thought? That Angelica was a guy.'"

"I guess that's why she came on so strong," Ephraim commented.

At least Sal was shook up enough to forget my next Killer's Delight and ask what I wanted.

I ordered my usual and dropped the change in Ephraim's cup.

CHAPTER 3 - THE QUEEN OF THE DEW DROP INNE

Sharon was the queen of the Dew Drop. Most of the women regulars were prematurely grizzled, baggy, and missing teeth. They looked as they were, longtime drinkers who had lived poor and hard. Sharon was different. She was pretty damn good-looking and not somebody you'd expect to find in a local hole of a bar. But there she was.

It was, she explained, a matter of finances and convenience. Sharon worked at the Gentle Ben's Club, one of those places that try for magical and end up at overpriced. She had been their cigarette and cigar girl and had made good money. Her legs, which were something special, long and ready to dance, had brought in the tips. Then the health crusaders in the capitol stopped the smoking in bars, restaurants, and clubs. She wasn't fired, but she was moved to the coatroom, where those legs couldn't do much for her. Worse, it was near the door, so on cold evenings she had to not wear the shorty skirts and fishnet stockings that served her so well.

Her reduced income meant Sharon had to give up her own clubbing. But, like the rest of us, she needed a place to drink and a place where people cared enough to remember her name. The Dew Drop was on the way between Ben's and her home, the drinks weren't watered, and, well, everybody wants to be a queen.

Sharon regularly sat a table two over from where Ephraim did his singing. Her chair, and nobody else ever sat on it, was the least beat-up in the Dew Drop. Most importantly, Sal actually waited on her. The rest of us had to serve ourselves; going up to the bar to order and carrying our drinks back to our various spots in the room. Deference can be made of simple gestures.

No wonder Sharon was pissed when Shelly brought this new girl, Monica, around. Monica was a woman worth noticing, not just for her legs, but also for her lilting laugh and easygoing way. What nobody could figure was what she was doing with Shelly.

Shelly explained, "I met her at work. She was doing some research."

"Research?"

"Yeah, that's what she does—research."

We wondered what kind of research would have brought a classy lady like Monica to Shelly's work. He was the projectionist at The Maxi Triple X, an old movie theater near the bus station. Once The Olympic and a majestic home of Oscar winners, The Maxi had long since been converted to four tiny auditoriums in which movies about multiple partners, big cocks, huge tits, and repetitive plots provided excuses for onanists, teenagers with fake identifications, and homeless guys with a buck and a need to get off the street for a few hours.

Shelly wasn't a regular regular at The Dew Drop and he smelled like stale cheese, which wasn't helped by his always wearing the same blue flannel work shirt and khaki pants. Still, we treated him like family. Every once in a while he'd invite a couple of us over to see one of the newer shows. We'd sneak a bottle of something into the projection room and enjoy a free movie and feel important, which was pretty cool in our world. So, like I said, Shelly was part of the family.

We wondered about Monica and research and all, but we didn't ask many questions and we didn't get any real answers.

"I didn't come here to talk about work," was all Monica would tell us that first day, "but I do know a good joke." Quickly, she had us laughing with the first of many dumb drunk jokes.

"An amnesiac comes into a bar. He asks, 'Do I come here often?"

Immediately, we were giggling away like a bunch of school kids.

She joked and regaled us, and we, enjoying her smiles and laughter, were quick to guffaw no matter how trite or meaningless the gag.

Of course, Sharon wasn't charmed, neither was she foolish enough to say anything. Instead, sizing up the situation, she went up to her new rival and asked, "Can I buy you a drink?"

"Yeah, thanks, sweetheart. I'll have a Bloody Mary."

Sharon actually went up to the bar and ordered. While Sal was making it, I could see the blood in Sharon's eyes.

Over the weeks it was weird how we regulars divided. There were those who focused on Sharon's legs and crowded around her in a now tight knot. Then there were the Monica devotees. I have to admit I was one of them; how could you not fall in love with that charm, with those gentle green eyes, with that happy laugh, and with that smile? Her breasts – C, but perfect beneath her sweater tops. May not have been as full as Sharon's; her ass may not have been quite so round; her legs may not have been quite so well shaped or cleansed of hair; but Monica was someone you could love, someone you could imagine cuddling up to in a warm bed, someone with whom you could imagine making a life.

Perhaps even more powerful was that ability to make us laugh. Monica told us more stupid jokes, and we, sad denizens of a liquid world, were only too happy to join in her merriment. The sharing of humor helped us, Monica's devotees, to overcome the potential issues of competitive lust and enter into a camaraderie in which our motto, if we had had one, might have been, "Monica for all and all for Monica."

We didn't see our "girlfriend" outside of the Dew Drop until one day Ephraim and I were walking from our rooming house to have one of those quick drinks before the next. There were a lot of days like that; days when the drinking started easy and got even easier, one glass following the next. With nothing else on our minds, wrapped in our jackets and balaclavas and leaning against the bitter December wind, we didn't take any notice of the big, dark Mercury, old but somehow classy, that pulled up beside us. Walking was effort enough.

The horn burped, and we jumped. "Guys, you want a ride?" Even muffled by weather and hat there was no mistaking that voice. Out attention was immediate and joyous; our response burbled and confused. In the end, Ephraim and his guitar in the back seat and I in the passenger's had the luxury of being limousined to our favorite bar.

Monica pulled up next to the Dew Drop and said; "I'll see you boys later."

"Aren't you coming in?"

"No, I have work that has to be done. I'll be back in a while."

"Thanks for the ride." Ephraim fumbled his guitar case out of the rear door.

For my part, I was torn. Sure I wanted a drink, but I didn't want to leave that car. I didn't want to have Monica driving off. I knew I would spend the afternoon thinking about her, wishing her return. I could feel Roger-Dodger, yeah, that's my name for him, it, getting excited, and I knew unrequited desire would be hot on my play list.

"Cal." My name sounded sweet on her lips. "I have to get going."

"Yeah, sorry. I just …" There really wasn't anything else. "Hey, have a great day." I tried to sound smooth. Opening the door, I stepped out and almost fell on my ass. Somebody had dumped some liquid on the sidewalk, and it had frozen.

"Shit." I grabbed the door, steadied myself, and smiled weakly.

"Take care of yourself." I imagined her deep concern.

"Yeah, you too."

Ephraim led the way in announcing, "Guess what?" as he entered. The five minutes of our ride in Monica's car would provide an afternoon of excited discussion. Every time the conversation waned, another regular would drift in. Etiquette demanded that each be told the day's big adventure. With each telling, the cold became less bearable, the car grew bigger and more comfortable, my near fall became more precarious, and Monica became sweeter and more beautiful. Even the sneers of the Sharon devotees couldn't dampen our adolescent enthusiasm.

Monica never drove that Mercury to The Dew Drop. "I don't ever drink and drive," she explained. We all nodded. Lots of the regulars had lost their licenses; a few had even been guests of the county. Even Sharon was forced to agree that it was better for Monica to leave her car at home.

As a result, Ephraim and I were the only ones who had seen the car before that one horrible day.

Monica wasn't laughing. She seemed to almost stumble into The Dew Drop. Her clothes were a bit disheveled, not torn or anything, just in disarray. She was rubbing her left cheek, high up, near the eye, where there was a red mark like she'd hit it against something. Mostly, she was using language that wasn't out of place in a bar but sure was out of place for her. Sal took one look and started making her a Bloody Mary.

"Two shots," she told him; and we all knew things were really bad.

"What happened?" Jonny had actually stopped his pool game. Now that was something.

"You won't believe it."

"What?" I tried to move closer, to put my arm around her.

I was surprised and cut off by Sharon. For the moment the bond of womanhood was stronger than the rivalry for top of the bar. "What's the matter, Sugar?" she crooned as if they had always been best friends.

"My car … I had an accident. It was out on Route 48. I was driving … This horse—"

A horse? Who the hell has a horse? I looked at Ephraim figuring if it had to do with horses his Amish background might come in handy. "A horse?" I asked out loud.

"Oh, he's fine. The bastard got up and jumped right back over that fence."

"You hit a horse?" Tony seemed to have gotten the idea first.

"Yeah. Would you believe it? Out of nowhere. He jumped the god-damned fence, and I was driving and—"

"How do you know it was a he?" Ray's question sounded as dumb as most of the things he said. This time nobody laughed; we just scowled at him as Sal brought Monica her drink.

"I don't know. I just know. The farmer, he called the fucker a he."

Most of us were startled by her language. Ray nodded as if this was important information.

"But you're all right?" I half asked and half stated. "I mean you aren't hurt or anything, are you?"

"I'm okay, but my car. I have a busted grille, and there's a leak—I'm not sure what, but something. Now I got to get it fixed, which means money I don't have. I don't know what—"

"Doesn't the horse's owner have to pay up?" Sal seldom involved himself in our conversations, but now we were on his favorite topic, money.

"No, not in this state. A farm animal gets on the highway; the farmer takes care of the animal, and the driver takes care of the damn car. That's the fuckin' law."

"Wow!' "Whoa!" "That's crazy."

"But that farmer did offer me something." She paused. "You won't believe this."

We waited in wondering anticipation. Finally, Sal asked her. "So what did he offer you?"

"He gave me a yak."

"A what?"

"A yak."

We buzzed for a minute.

Finally, Jonny explained with some authority that there really were some yaks raised in the state. "They're raised for milk," he told us. "It makes great cheese – especially mozzarella." I had no idea how he knew about yaks and all, but he sounded sure of himself, and Monica was even listening to him like she was learning something. Which was all very well and good, but didn't make the rest of us feel any better; it wasn't like we were making Monica's problem go away.

"Let's take a look at the car," I offered. It wasn't as if I knew anything about cars and motors and leaks, but I certainly had nothing to say about big hairy beasts that should have been roaming the Himalayas.

We pulled on our jackets and went outside. There it was, big, dark, and bashed in the front. We fumbled around until Chip got the bright idea of getting in and he found the lever to open the hood. It took a bit before Tony got it securely propped open so we weren't going to get our collective heads bashed. Then we gathered around the motor, our heads hovering, our hands groping stupidly, and all the while making what were supposed to sound like intelligent comments.

"Radiator fluid."

"Maybe the brakes?"

"No, power steering."

"Are you sure it isn't the oil?"

"Nah, oil is more bluish." Ray was carefully examining the fluid quickly freezing on his fingertips. "But it sure is something."

We stood there groping in helplessness, catching fingers and scraping knuckles. Yapping meaningless oaths, our collective breath provided a steaming cloud.

"Guys. Hey guys, mind if I take your pictures?" At some point Monica had pulled a camera from the back seat.

Of course none of us objected, so she snapped away.

Feeling like he'd lost the momentum, Jonny asked loudly. "So what are you gonna do with that yak?"

Knowing I wasn't going to fix that car and neither were the others, I figured the yak might actually be a good idea. "Yeah, Monica, are you going to keep in at your place?"

"No, the farmer will raise it. When he sells it, I get the money – minus his cost. He says I may make a grand."

"No foolin'." For the first time I realized that even Sal had come out to the car.

"Hey, Sal, maybe you could raise a couple out back."

"Ha, ha." He turned to go back in. "Yous guys drinkin' or what?"

We hesitated for a moment, torn between Monica, who was still snapping pictures of us, her car, and the front of The Dew Drop, and the drinks that waited within. Finally, defeated by nothing, we retreated back into the bar.

Monica didn't follow.

"We'll see ya," I called to Monica with a wave.

"Ya, see you guys," she responded.

***

Sundays The Dew Drop opened at two, which meant most of us would be waiting on the sidewalk when Sal would show up. We'd stand like salivating dogs waiting for dinner while he'd open the door and then push our way in behind him while the lights were still flickering on.

That next Sunday Sharon also showed up right at two, which was unusual. We didn't usually see her on the Sabbath, something about her childhood and religion. But that Sunday she was there carrying "The Monthly Rag." It was a local feminist newspaper, one devoted to putting down men. She walked in and threw it down on the pool table, scattering balls and evoking some cursing.

"What the fuck?" Jonny, who was already racking the balls for his first game, demanded.

"Take a look at this," she said. "Take a fuckin' look at this." She'd found the page she wanted. There were pictures of The Dew Drop, and of us—the bunch of us standing around looking like idiots. It was one of those local color things. This one was titled "Could These Local Men Survive on Mars?" It was written by somebody named Muriel Seachrest, who'd gone underground to see how dumb a bunch of average guys, the kind of guys who hung out in a neighborhood bar, could be.

She had written about The Dew Drop and how none of us knew about cars, but acted like we did. The liquid, which she had dumped on the ground herself, was, and this really hurt, cheap vodka mixed with water and a little grease from a burger joint.

To add to her fun, she wrote about the damn yak, which had never existed. But if it had, its milk wouldn't have been used to make mozzarella. "Good mozzarella," the article explained, "is made from the milk of water buffalo." Turns out that yak are raised here, but for meat and their hair, which makes great sweaters.

She made us sound gullible and full of ourselves, which I guess was true. The most gullible had been Ephraim and me. We're the ones who had seen the car first, that dark green Mercury, so we really felt dumb when she pointed out that the car she had brought to the bar that day, the one that was busted up, was a black Lincoln. I mean how stupid were we?

Her conclusion: "When men don't know anything, it's easiest for them to make believe they know a lot." That really stung.

We knew we'd probably never see Monica or Muriel, whichever was her real name, again, certainly not at The Dew Drop. The next time Shelly came in, we asked why he hadn't warned us. He looked sheepish and said that was the way it was.

"So did she write about the Maxi?" Tony asked.

Shelly turned a bit red as he pulled a paper from his wallet. He unfolded it and smoothed it onto the table. The headline said it all: "Men Who Love Their Hands."

No one wanted to go any farther; we didn't want to lose those free visits to The Maxi Triple X. The whole subject was dropped. You can only go so far with embarrassment, but every now and then somebody would replay the joke Sharon told us that Sunday, the joke she had told us after we had all had a chance to read that story and to look at our pictures in the paper. She told it like the queen she was—without inflection or explanation. When she finished, we didn't laugh; neither did she. It was the only joke Sharon ever told, but every now and then, one of us would repeat it—just to remind ourselves.

"An elephant sees a camel passing by and tells her, 'How funny, you have your tits on your back.' The camel, stares at him calmly for a moment and answers, 'That's quite a strange remark from someone who's got his dick on his forehead!'"

CHAPTER 4 - THE VETERAN

We looked down on Ray. He was a panhandler, and that was beneath us. But we put up with him because he was a veteran. At least that's what it said on the cardboard sign he carried. Trish, who would help out anyone, had made if for him, carefully blocked lettering with a Magic Marker on a piece of cardboard box.

INJURED VETERAN

PLEASE HELP

GOD BLESS YOU

He had wanted more words. "It don't look like the signs the other guys carry," Ray complained.

"Don't worry about that. This one is easier to read," Trish had explained.

When Ray kept complaining, she said, "I can make you another one if this one doesn't work. Give it a try."

The next day Ray said he'd done well. He even offered to buy Trish a drink.

It wasn't really clear that Ray was a veteran. He'd been in the army; that much was true. He'd joined up right out of high school. He hadn't graduated, just been given a school leaving certificate, which meant there wasn't much more he or they could do. His stepfather, who had been happy to be rid of him, had suggested joining up. The counselor at the high school had been skeptical. The recruiter had been worried about making his quota. In the end, Ray had gone off to boot camp.

About three weeks in, he had been injured. It wasn't that he'd done something bad—only that he'd done something badly. They'd been out on an obstacle course, one with explosions and live ammunition for effect. "Keep down," the sergeant had shouted as the men crawled on their bellies under barbed wire.

Ray's boot had caught on something. Instead of backing up, Ray had lifted himself off the ground. "Just a little," he explained to us, "but I guess it was too much. Boy was the Sarge pissed." The bullet had caught him in the heel. "Darn near wrecked it," was Ray's description.

"I hadn't wanted to leave the army. I liked it. 'Specially the food.

Never got nowhere near that much to eat at home, not with the eight of us."

"Your folks had six kids?" I asked having done some quick math.

"Hell no. 'Tween 'em they had fourteen of us. There was just eight of us still at home before I left. So thar was never 'nough to eat.

"Anyways the army said I couldn't fight no more on account of my heel so they gave me what they calls a general discharge. I don't get no benefits or nothing, 'cept if the foot needs workin' on.

"They did say I might get some help with schoolin', but that didn't seem likely. Havin' part of my foot shot off weren't gonna make me no smarter."

Ray started laughing at himself, so we all joined in. He laughed at himself a lot and that made him one of the family. That was one thing about Ray; he was always smiling and laughing. It would have been hard to not like the guy.

Ray never did a mean thing, but he never did anything right either.

From time to time one of us would try to get him a job. I asked Chan to let him help clean the dumpster. Okay, it was for myself—I hated that part of my job, but I did figure it would help Ray out.

Ray managed to get garbage all over the alley and the back walkway from Chan's to the dumpster. It took me three hours of cleaning and mopping to get it right again. Worse, Chan didn't want to pay me.

"You brought pig to sty. Now you clean sty up," he had argued.

I told him he wasn't being fair. He said he'd pay me half. I figured that was as good a deal as I was getting. After that I never tried to help Ray again.

Even Sal felt sorry for the guy. One day he told Ray he could clean the bathroom for a couple of drinks. "I learned how to do that in the army," Ray had enthused.

The plumber who unclogged the toilet didn't say much, just shook his head and demanded fifty bucks. Given Sal's feelings about money, that must have really hurt. What added insult was Ray had already downed those drinks before Chip had gone to use the john. When the water had poured onto the floor and Chip had come swearing out the bathroom door, Ray had asked, "Hey, Sal, want to give me another drink, and I'll mop that up?"

Ray was always telling the rest of us how much he'd loved being in the army—how much, yes how much he wished he'd been able to stay.

"What did the army think about you?" Ephraim asked him one day.

"Oh, they liked me real good. The sergeant told me I was a real good soldier 'cause I did what I was told and I never did think about nothin'."

CHAPTER 5 - SIDEWINDER

A stranger limped into The Dew Drop one fall day. He was favoring his left leg and leaning on a stick, whittled fancy with a rattlesnake curling around it. Tall, lank, black hair tied back, eyes that belied his pleased-to-meet-you smile, and black Stetson hat that sat high on his head; he called for a tequila boilermaker from half way to the bar. It was one of those acts of braggadocio that tell you right off this guy is going to be fun or trouble—more likely both.

Maybe Sal was looking to see if this stranger showed signs of money, but the rest of us were focused on that hat and especially its band—a rattler's skin complete with seven rattles.

"Name's Cody," he said as he sat on a stool, pulled a twenty out of his pocket and slapped it on the bar.

"Yous want a drink?"

"That's the idea, partner." He pushed the twenty toward Sal.

"Enjoys yourself," Sal said as he put down a shot and a glass of beer; the new guy took the shot in one gulp and followed it with a long draught of beer. "Another one, if you don't mind."

Rotating on his stool, he smiled at Tony, stuck out his hand and said, "Hi, I'm Cody."

Tony took the proffered hand and mumbled his own name.

"Tony, good to meet ya, Tony. Can I buy ya a drink?"

Immediately Cody was everybody's friend.

He turned his attention to that second shot, tossed it back, and set his hat on the stool next to him. Ephraim was picking at a song, one I'd never heard before, something about mowing a meadow and being bit by a snake. Cody smiled. "You like my hat band?"

"I certainly do," Ephraim half reached for the hat as if he expected Cody to pass it to him. Instead, he plunked it back on his own head and launched into a story.

"There's this little town in Arizona, almost a ghost town. Name's Crown King. Maybe forty houses. Nice little saloon, only real business in town, but it does right well.

"Now I'm in that bar one Sunday afternoon. I'd been hired to work on this guy's place—needed a new roof. I'm tossing back a few and enjoying the folks there. They're talkin' 'bout how they'd dynamite the bridge on the main road inta town if too many folks were to try and come in. Ya know, like some big disaster down in Phoenix or something. I mean these guys are acting like they're mountain men. Anyhow, one of these assholes looks down on the floor right under his stool; Goddamn if there ain't this big old rattler just curled up there. I mean the door's open and there weren't nothin' to keep him out, but I sure don't know what he's drinkin'.

"Anywise, these wannabe mountain men, they all freeze up. The guy who's sittin' on that stool—well, he's about as pale as a man can get and still be upright. Not me, I ain't afraid of no snake; my daddy used to hunt them, sell 'em to all kinds of different places—some dead and some live.

"So I know just what to do, and I do it. I stomp down on that snake, just behind his head and take out my knife." At this point he pulls out a mean looking knife he's got tucked in the small of his back.

"I whack off that snake's head fast and proceed to skin the fucker right there and then. All these guys are watchin' me. Couple ask if I want to sell that skin, but I say, 'No thanks.' I figure it'll make a great hatband, and here it is." He took off the hat and held it out for us to see more clearly, slowly rotating it.

"I did let them keep the head and the meat. Don't know what they did with it; I kept what I wanted." He smiled and ran his hand around the hat brim.

***

Ephraim and I were walking home from The Dew Drop that evening. He let out a slow whistle and stopped in the middle of Rose Street. "I don't trust that guy," he commented. "I don't trust him at all. Strikes me he's a sidewinder if ever I met one."

He didn't say any more, just took up walking again, his usual even gait, his guitar case bumping against his right leg as we moved along. When we got back to our rooming house, Ephraim stopped in the hallway, "Mark my words, I'm telling you right now, that guy's a sidewinder."

I didn't particularly share Ephraim's dislike of Cody, but I certainly didn't like him the way most of the others did. He was one of these guys who have lots of brag and take charge, but never quite seem to have much get it done.

One thing he talked us all into was a potluck supper. We decided to hold it the last Tuesday of the month, which meant a couple days before Thanksgiving. It seemed like a good idea, a bit of a Thanksgiving, a sort of celebration of our own little family. Even Sal got into the spirit and agreed to spring for the first beer for every participant. "Yous just got to bring something for everybody else, you know maybe enough for ten people. Everybody bring something, and I'll throw yous a beer. Fair enough?"

We all nodded in agreement.

Ephraim decided to make cookies and asked Mrs. Buthyre, our landlady, if he could use the kitchen. She said okay, but as time got short, he decided buying a bag of Chips Ahoy and dumping them into a plastic bag would be easier.

At the time I had a part-time job at Heinrich's Real Deli. I came in some nights and mopped the floors, washed pots and pans and containers, cleaned the counters—that kind of stuff. It wasn't hard work, and I managed to swipe some good stuff for Ephraim and me to eat. The only thing I knew I had to stay away from was the beer. Magda, Heinrich's wife, knew I liked my beer so she kept careful count.

I figured Monday night I'd just help myself to a couple pounds of potato salad. I was kind of worried Heinrich might notice if I took too much of one thing, so I planned to take some German and some regular and maybe some egg salad and mix them all together.

When it came time to actually take the salad, I thought, what the fuck, and helped myself to extra German for Mrs. Buthyre. It never hurts to gild things a bit.

Ephraim and I got to The Dew Drop at five thirty, him carrying a plastic bag of cookies and me with my tub from Heinrich's. Sal took our contributions and served each of us a glass of Bud. "After this yous pay, right?"

"Right," Ephraim echoed. I just nodded.

We weren't the first ones there. Already it was obvious there was a problem. Cookies, brownies, loaves of bread, potato salad and more potato salad, macaroni salad, too; carbohydrates were everywhere, but nothing else. No vegetables and no meat, not even a burger or a hotdog.

Sharon showed up. She had brought a sheet cake, white cake with red frosting and a butter cream turkey right in the middle. She told us she'd baked it herself, but I whispered to Ephraim, "I didn't know Sharon did her baking at Albertsons."

He grinned and punched me in the arm.

Sharon must have heard me, because she smiled and said, "Hold that pose, you two."

"Huh?" Ephraim and I answered as one.

She pulled out a camera, one of those throwaways. "Hit him again," she instructed. Ephraim did as he was told with all the spontaneity gone. She snapped and announced, "I'm documenting the fun so you drunks can remember it."

There were a few groans and some laughs as she took more pictures.

Carol, who as usual was wearing enough makeup for a troop of clowns, had brought mustard, ketchup, and relish. Most likely she had swiped them from the restaurant where she waitressed. She'd also brought her brother, Mike, a cop. Being a cop, Mike didn't usually drink at neighborhood joints like The Dew Drop, but that night he came with Carol—even bringing a couple of packages each of hotdog and hamburger rolls.

Cody, hat perched high on his head and stick in hand, was one of the last to arrive. He, too, had brought carbs, his in the form of baked beans. "Real cowboy beans," he announced. They were in a tinfoil pan; I figured he'd opened a few cans. But that wasn't all he'd done; he'd dumped in some Tabasco. Jesus, what a kick! I took a mouthful and grabbed one of those hamburger rolls, stuffing it into my burning mouth. Meanwhile, that damn sidewinder laughed at me like I was some kind of asshole. As luck would have it, just as I was tasting those beans, Sharon had her trusty Kodak pointed in my direction and caught the entire sequence.

We ate a lot of crap and drank even more beer, and the hard stuff. Sal more than made his investment of a glass of draught for each of us back.

The conversation went round and round; then it started to peter out. It was probably time to quit, but most of us didn't want to stop drinking.

"Hey, Cody," Al shouted even though they were right next to each other.

"What?" Cody shouted back.

"Why don't you tell everybody about that rattlesnake."

"Why?" He sounded querulous. "I've told you guys a hundred times."

"It's a good story, and some people haven't heard it." Al looked around for a moment. "Mike, you haven't heard it, have you?"

"Nope."

Cody shuffled and aw-geed a bit; but once he got started, it was all theater. At the end, he took the hat off and passed it to Mike, who examined it gravely before he commented. "I notice you like to wear this high, like it's a bit small for you."

Cody shrugged like that meant nothing, but I was pretty sure he was burnt. "I like it that way," he muttered and shifted his weight from foot to foot.

"That must have been before you hurt your leg?" None of us had ever thought about it before, but it would have taken some fancy footwork to stomp that snake.

"Yeah, it was. I was up on a roof, and the damn thing gave way. Busted my leg real bad. Wouldn't go racin' a rattler now." Cody tried to make his voice matter-of-fact, but it was obvious that Mike had hit another sore spot. He yawned a bit theatrically and said, "I guess it's time for me to be goin'; got a job of work tomorrow."

"Not on a roof, I hope," Mike responded.

"No, I don't do roofin' no more."

Cody reached out for his hat, and Mike gave it back. "That's quite a story." He, too, looked ready to leave.

Cody left first, limping on that stick of his, his jacket pulled tight and that hat pulled down as low as he could get it against the wind.

"Yous forgot your beans," Sal called after him. The door closed. "Shit, guess I got to take them out to the garbage."

"I'll do it for you," I offered. I started gathering the debris from the party. Ephraim and Ray joined in. Soon, The Dew Drop was back to its normal state of dump.

For a few days we talked about the potluck making it more than it was, but mostly just reassuring ourselves that it had been fun. Slowly, it dimmed as a topic of conversation.

Then Sharon showed up with her photos and tacked them up on a wall. That got us talking all over again. Ephraim especially liked the one of me with my mouth stuffed with hamburger roll and tears streaming down my face. He kept going back to look at it and laugh.

Another favorite was one of Sal. I'd missed that moment. Sharon had cut that butter cream turkey out of the middle of her Albertson's cake and served it to him. There he was with a forkful of goop on the way to his mouth and looking like a kid at a birthday party.

Carol asked if she could take one of the pictures for her brother. It was toward the end of the party when Cody was telling his story. It was a good picture of the both of them, and we all agreed that Mike should have it as a memento.

Two days later, Ephraim and I were surprised to find Mike and another guy we'd never seen sitting at a table and drinking beer. We looked at Sal, who shrugged. "Hey," I called out, and Mike waved in response.

Sal had his favorite, Waylon Jennings, playing on the sound system. That system was a scratchy, crackling affair, not something you'd use for music, which was one reason we all liked to have Ephraim around.

"For God's sake turn that crap off and let Ephraim play something," Tim yelled. Tim was not somebody whom you'd expect to yell, but he must have been at The Dew Drop for a couple of hours, and there's only so much static a man can stand.

"Yous want a drink?" Sal asked me as he switched off the music. He knew better than to ask Ephraim. As usual, his first beer would come when a buck sixty had been dropped in his bowl.

It must have been half an hour before Cody came by. "Hey, Cody, let me buy you a beer," Mike yelled across the room. "I got this buddy I want you to meet." He turned to his companion, "That there's Cody, the guy I was telling you 'bout. Get a load of that hatband. Would you believe he killed that rattler right there on a bar floor?"

The other man nodded gravely. "Where did you say that was?"

"Shit, I forget; what town was that, someplace in Arizona wasn't it?"

"Yeah, Crown King, just a little place; ever hear of it?" Cody took the glass of beer Sal had poured.

Cody might have reached into his pocket for the money, but Sal stopped him, "Yous heard the man, he's buyin'."

Cody limped across the bar to the chair that Mike had pulled out. "Sit down and tell my buddy, Jack, that story. I'm tellin' you, Jack, it's really something."

No sooner had Cody set himself down then there were two guns at his head and a hand on each shoulder.

"Now, Mr. Cody Jackson, real easy like, you lean forward and let me relieve you of that knife you're carrying." Mike hissed the words, and there was no question he was ready to pull the trigger if need be.

Ephraim and I stopped breathing.

Tim ducked down in the corner behind his table. Then he reached back up to grab his beer.

Once Cody had been searched, cuffed, and read his rights, the two cops dragged him out.

The Dew Drop was dead quiet. Nothing kills a place like the cops arresting a guy.

"Crap," Sal suddenly exclaimed, "they didn't pay for that beer."

We all laughed, and the conversation picked up a little. But the effect didn't last. It was a quiet evening. We drank, but the alcohol didn't lift the mood. As other regulars came in, those who had been there told and retold the story, but nobody had an explanation.

"What the fuck was that about?" we asked over and over.

***

A few days passed; then Mike stopped in. "Sal, I want to pay you for that glass of beer."

"Forget it," Sal answered; but we all knew he wanted the lousy money.

Mike put the right amount on the bar. With a shrug, Sal gathered it up and dropped the money into the till. "Are yous gonna tell us what?"

"I guess you got a right." Mike settled himself on a stool.

"Yous want a beer?"

"No, thanks." Mike laid his hands flat on the bar top. "That guy

Jack?"

"Yeah," I answered for everybody.

"He was here from the Arizona state police. They got a few warrants on that fella. Him and his cousin, Jefferson Jackson, were in Crown King and they got some little fame 'cause Jefferson—not that Cody faker—did kill a sidewinder. That much was a true story.

"They weren't doing any roofing or anything honest though. Nope, they were roaming the small towns of Nevada, Utah, Arizona, and I guess next would have been New Mexico, looking for places to rob. Gas stations, general stores, you know those little places where they could grab some money, cigarettes, beer, food and take off. They were probably scoping out that Saloon when that snake thing happened; so Jefferson must have figured he'd settle for that skin. Did a nice job of it, too.

"Couple weeks later they hit a general store in another town." Mike looked like he was searching for the name. "Bumble Bee. Yeah, that was the name; I kind of liked the sound of it, but Jack told me there's nothin' much there, just a general store. The fellow who owns it got to be at least ninety."

"No shit!" Sal said. I couldn't help wondering how many years he expected to be running The Dew Drop.

Mike went on, "So these two figured it would be an easy job—just this old geezer. What they didn't know ..." Here he took a long breath. "What they didn't know was this old geezer had a Glock 39 strapped to his hip. The guy's old, but turns out he's a crack shot. He puts one between Jefferson's eyes. Drops him right there.

"Our hero Cody starts to run, turns back and grabs his cousin's hat." Mike took a minute to scratch his head. "Then he takes off like a rabbit.

"Well the old guy figures the cops might not like two dead bodies as much as a fugitive to hunt down, so he puts one in his leg, which is—"

"Why he limps," Tim finished for him.

"Which is why he limps," Mike repeated.

"But how'd yous guys know?" Sal demanded.

"Just one of those cop things. We get flyers; we get 'em all the time. Look at 'em. Forget 'em. But this one, the snake skin; it just wasn't something that totally slips away. I might have forgotten the whole thing, you know, it wasn't like a big deal or anything. But then my sister brought me that picture, which made me think on it again.

"Well, I said what the hell and sent it on to Arizona asking if it was their guy. Next thing I know, Jack is in town asking to go bar hopping."

Mike stood up and stretched. "I guess I'd better get back." He shook hands with a few of us and walked out.

We sat quiet for a few minutes and then went back to our usual. Before he resumed his singing, Ephraim commented. "Nothing good ever comes from a sidewinder's braggin'."

I nodded agreement and flat out bought him his first beer of the day.

CHAPTER 6 - PICNIC

Some days are just too good to have a hangover. This one started with the light that came around the shades and the smell and feel of the air that came through the window. It was a crisp, comfortable air that made me want to breathe. Then there were the sounds—especially the calls of the birds. Strange how on some days all you hear is the caw of angry crows and on others, like this one, there are sweet songs and contented coos. I could even hear the insects, not annoying buzzes and hums, but productive insects scurrying about their day.

Days like that are enough to make a drunk want to puke, or maybe, just maybe, do something out of the ordinary.

Ephraim and I met at the bathroom door. We were usually the last of the five boarders at Mrs. Buthyre's rooming house to get up. We were also typically the last two to get in at night. If we weren't picking up a few bucks doing one dumb job or another, we were sure to be closing The Dew Drop. The night before had been a fun one at our favorite bar. We'd drunk more than usual and were more hung over than even we were used to. Still, it was one of those days, one of those get-out and enjoy days.

We washed and then sat in my room having another smoke to kill the aftertaste of the night. I'd pulled up the shade and opened the window as wide as it went. Ephraim stood looking out at Carlisle's Church of Redemption. It was a redbrick storefront with parking in the rear. Out front Carlisle—that was the preacher's name—had one of those church signboards. On this morning it read:

I CHRIST DOESN'T WANT YOU, CAR ISLES ILL DOES.

On the church's left was a Quickie Mart, which was one of the great attractions for those of us who roomed in Mrs. Buthyre's. On its right was an empty storefront with boarded windows and a beat-down appearance that proclaimed: This is the part of town for losers. Christ wouldn't be caught dead here.

"We ought to do something good today." Ephraim had caught my mood before I had a chance to say a word. That was often the way between us—two guys from totally different ends of the world who ended up in the same place physically and psychologically. Sometimes it felt like we were long-lost brothers who'd stumbled on each other.

"Yeah," I grunted agreement.

"What do you think?"

"I don't know." There was a pause like we were both thinking. "You got any ideas?"

"Nah ... but we should do somethin'."

"Yeah."

We lit up another pair of smokes. I liked Marlboros; I don't know what Ephraim liked. We both smoked Broncos because they were cheaper.

"When I was a kid —"

"Yeah?"

"Before my mother took off." He took a long draw on that smoke. "Before everything went to shit." Another drag. "On days like this she'd say 'Let's have a picnic,' and she'd load up that basket with good food. Viands was her word, not food — viands.

"She was one great cook. We'd have chicken and cornbread and pie, good old-fashioned fruit pies — my favorite was brambleberry, boy was that good. And we'd have applesauce and bean salad, and all kinds of stuff. And, yeah, the bread. She could bake bread that would melt right in your mouth. You didn't even need butter, but we had that, too, the sweetest butter you ever ate."

By this point he had my mouth watering and my mind trying to remember a picnic from when I was a kid. Trouble was, there hadn't been any, so I just nodded my head along with his talk. When he finished, I asked the only sensible question I could, "What'd you drink?"

"Not beer," he half laughed his answer. "We had spring water, and milk straight from our cows, and lemonade. My ma made the best lemonade you'd ever taste." He stopped for a moment. "Course now I'd probably like it better with some vodka in it."

"Or maybe tequila," I added for him.

"Yeah, maybe tequila."

"Anyway, Ephraim, that's one great idea. Let's have a picnic."

It took us a good hour to delegate the work. I was going to do the food, and Ephraim was going to come up with the liquid refreshments.

He took off for the Bevmo. I checked out what I had in the little, chipped fridge that came with the room, and walked over to that Quickie Mart counting the money I had left after that fun night at The Dew Drop. It wasn't much.

Ephraim returned with a large paper sack. He had two sixes of Colt. "I know, I know," he said before I could get a word out, "but it was on sale." He stopped for a moment and added, "I wanted to save a little extra to get these." He pulled out three bottles of lemonade. "It kind of makes me feel like home." He put everything back in the sack and tucked it into my refrigerator. I didn't have anything in there, which was good since that bag just about filled it.

I ducked my head in recognition and continued making our lunch.

My buddy sat on the bed—kind of tossing the blanket back in place before sitting. I was in the only usable chair, sitting at the small phony oak table that matched the warped set of drawers. Our rooms came furnished.

There was a second chair. It had a loose leg that was always threatening to give way. And there was a night table that was scarred and stained enough to be a hand-me-down from a whorehouse. In every room there was a picture, the same picture, one of those bleeding-heart-of-Jesus things that made no sense in a cheap boarding house. Mrs. Buthyre insisted they stay on the walls—kind of like Jesus was watching over us— and there was a mirror. Mine cracked and losing its silvering so I always looked like I was drunk and dying even on the good days.

I had a loaf of sandwich bread, some bologna that Herb at the Quickie had cut extra thin just for me, and some Kraft American slices. Herb had also cut a tomato into five roughly even slices. When Ephraim came back, I was spreading mustard and mayo on twelve slices of that soft, gooey bread. I was using packets I'd taken from the Quickie fixin's table while Herb was getting my order.

I was using one and a half slices of meat and one of cheese along with a slice of tomato in each sandwich. I'd figured on making five. Then I'd make one more with just bologna and cheese. I'd eat that one, and we'd have three each, which would be a real feast.

And then there was my surprise. I'd walked over to McDonald's and bought a couple of those gluey, apple pie things. They weren't brambleberry, but they would do.

I put the sandwiches and some napkins in a bag. When Ephraim wasn't looking, I threw those apple pie things in, too. Pulling the bag of drinks out of the fridge, I put in the leftover bread and cheese to keep it safe from bugs and other animal life.

"Let's do it," I said with as much gaiety as I could raise. I clapped Ephraim on the shoulder and handed him the bag of liquid refreshments.

"Yeah, but where are we going?" It wasn't something we had discussed. It wasn't something I had even considered. We stared blankly at each other with not an idea between us.

Finally, Ephraim asked, "Isn't there a park around here?"

"Yeah, but it's full of derelicts and winos."

"Oh." We went back to staring.

"There's another park," I suggested, "over on Miller. It isn't perfect, but it's better. Cleaner and all."

"Oh," his voice brightened.

It was a longer walk than either of us wanted; but we didn't have bus fare, so we hoofed it. I wanted to stop for one of those brews.

"Let's wait 'til we get to the park."

"How come?" I asked, feeling put out.

"It won't be a real picnic if we start in drinking." Ephraim sounded so eager that I gave in. We trudged on. My thoughts of a great day sullenly turned to *I want a drink*.

We arrived at Memorial Park. Surly as I had become, I did have to admit it was a better place. Not to say there weren't any derelicts around, but fewer and hopefully not so likely to start asking for a brew or a sandwich.

We scouted for a suitable spot. What we needed most was some bushes right nearby so we could stow that sack of beer out of sight. If a cop came by, he wouldn't see the whole stash. I wasn't planning on drinking that lemonade, but we'd leave it out—another way to fool that possible cop.

We found what seemed like a good enough spot, even with a tree to lean against. But it was kind of close to the playground, and I figured some mother might complain. "Move along, boys, move along!" I could hear the voice in blue in my head. So move along we did.

Finally, after what seemed like eternity without a drink, we found a spot that worked. Not near anything anyone would mind, a couple of bushes at hand filled with discarded cans and broken bottles, but good for stowing. "We can collect some of these cans," Ephraim said.

I'd been thinking the same thing, but we both knew the way the world works. "If it isn't somebody else's spot." Bums and drunks have their own rules. Ownership of can-scavenging spots is sacred.

"If nobody comes to work it," Ephraim corrected himself.

"Yeah, if…"

We settled on the grass, the sack of food between us, the lemonade bottles on display, and two cans of Colt carefully tucked into the curves of our bodies. Much as I wanted that brew, and I knew Ephraim did, too, neither of us took a swig. It was like a special moment, like we were anticipating something really grand and at the same time knew the reality could never measure up.

"Shit."

"Yeah, shit," I echoed. We opened our cans and took deep draughts. I reached in the bag, pulled out a sandwich, and handed it to him.

"Thanks."

"Welcome."

"Hey, mister." We hadn't noticed them. There they were right behind us, watching us with starving eyes and too much sadness—a mother and her three jetsam kids. The oldest looked to be a girl, maybe eight or nine. Her clothes way too big and in desperate need of a wash. The younger two seemed about the same age, maybe twins, a girl and what must have been the scrawniest little guy I'd ever seen—so thin his eyes seemed to take his entire face. He was the one talking.

"Can you spare some food?"

The woman looked away in shame while the older kid kind of pawed the ground and tried to not stare at the sandwich Ephraim was holding in front of his mouth.

"Charlie, that ain't proper," the woman said all the while somehow acknowledging that she had told him to ask.

"Yes'm." He tried to smile. The effort made those eyes grow.

I heard Ephraim kind of gasp and knew exactly how he was feeling. "These your children?" I asked, giving her the opportunity she so obviously wanted.

"This here's Charlie," she replied putting her hand on the boy's rag-mop head. "His sister, Darlene. They twins, but Darlene don't talk so much." She smiled, revealing stubs of brown and broken teeth. "And this is my oldest, Ruthann."

"Say howdy, children," she instructed.

"Howdy," the boy and his older sister echoed. Darlene just stared and stared hard at that sandwich.

"What do you think?" Ephraim whispered. The little girl took the smallest step forward.

"What about you?" I asked him back already knowing his answer.

"I'd feel awful guilty."

"Yeah, me, too." We looked at each other for a moment. It was seconds, but I could feel the tension mounting in those little bodies.

From the corner of my eye, I watched the woman. Her body seemed to sag beneath the weight of her ill-fitting clothes. She oozed helplessness and resignation. "What's your name?"

"Lucile, not that it matters."

"It matters," I replied. "I like knowing who I'm breaking bread with." With that I gestured for them to come closer.

They shuffled toward us with looks of disbelief, fear and anticipation.

I had regrets as soon as they got close enough to smell. *How long has it been since they've had a bath?*

Ephraim held out that first sandwich to the older girl, who started to rip it into parts. "No, that one's for you," he said as he reached into the bag for a second and then a third.

I took one out and gestured it toward Lucile. It seemed to take all her restraint to hold back. "Are you sure?"

"We have plenty. Luckily, I got kind of carried away in the kitchen."

They held the sandwiches, looking at them almost like they were afraid to take a bite. I pulled another sandwich out and handed it to Ephraim and then the last one for myself. Smiling, I took a big bite and started chewing.

They followed suit, standing there, taking small bites and chewing carefully, trying to make the moment last.

"Sit down," Ephraim suggested. They seemed to nod in unison but continued standing.

"Would the children like some lemonade?" I asked feeling foolish to ask a question with such an obvious answer.

Lucile stopped chewing. "I'd think so."

I patted the ground and then opened the first bottle. Charlie plunked himself down on the spot I'd patted. I handed him the yellow liquid and he started to drink. "Charlie, where are your manners?" the woman demand.

"Yes'm," he responded. He mumbled, "Thank you, sir," and took another sip before I could answer.

Ruthann took Darlene by the hand and sat her down next to her brother. She said nothing as I put another bottle in her hand. Lucile didn't say anything about manners and clearly Darlene was going to remain mute.

"You, too," I said to Ruthann, who thanked me even before she sat. "You're very welcome." I handed over her bottle.

"That's right kind of you," Lucile said with such a tone of pain that I might just as well have been torturing her children.

"I'm afraid we don't have any more lemonade," Ephraim spoke up. "Would you care for one of these?" He held his can of Colt aloft.

"If you can spare," her tone suddenly lifted.

He got to his feet and walked over to the bushes. He came back with a can for her and a replacement. "You ready for one?" he eyeballed me.

I finished off my first in one gulp, threw the empty at him, and muttered, "Yep." Handing me the replacement, he went back to the bush for another.

We were a happy, if wordless group of picnickers. The children nursed their food and their drink. Between bites and swallows they'd take careful looks to see how much was left. Darlene was the last to finish. When the final morsel was gone, she looked like she might start in crying.

"I've got a surprise for you kids," I said. I pulled out those McDonalds' pies and broke them into halves. I gave each of the kids a half and the last to Lucile.

She wanted it. I could see she wanted it bad. But she handed it to Ruthann. "For you kids."

"Yes'm." The girl thought for a moment, looked at her brother, who ever so slightly nodded in agreement to something unsaid, and then handed that last half to Darlene. It was a moment sweet, sad, full of love. I wanted to do more, something, but knew there was nothing. I could feel tears starting to well, and I figured Ephraim would be feeling them, too.

When the malt liquor was gone, I put all the empties in one of the bags and handed it to Ruthann. "You can turn these in and get some money."

"I know. Thank you." She spoke so softly that I had to strain to hear. "We usually get the ones in those bushes."

"Oh, it's your spot?"

She ducked her head in response. "Well, we'll get out of your way." Somehow a new and different discomfort had found its way into Ephraim's voice. We had interfered with their routine, with their way of life. That wasn't how things were supposed to be—not in our world.

Clumsily he and I got up. "I guess we'll be going," I announced.

"Okay," Lucile answered in a tired voice that said go and stay at the same time.

"Thanks for the cans," Ruthann said.

"Thanks for lunch," her mother added as if from some sudden memory.

"Thanks for lunch," Charlie and his older sister echoed.

It was Ephraim and my turn to bob our heads.

We got about sixty or seventy yards before a cop stopped us. "Hold up, you two." He was a young guy, probably pretty new to the force. He was holding a bicycle with his left hand and kind of fingering his stick with his right. I tensed and wished I could run but knew it was useless.

"Officer?" I asked, scared shit and subservient.

"We weren't doing nothing," Ephraim half whined.

"I was watching you two." His voice was even, no sign of anger or beat-down. "That family come here every day?" It was a question, but he obviously knew the answer.

"I think so, to collect the cans. I guess they need the money."

"Right." His voice seemed almost gentle this time. "They must be homeless."

"Yeah." This time Ephraim answered.

"You guys feed them?" Again one of those questions that didn't really need answering.

"They looked hungry."

"I saw." He reached in his pocket, took out a wallet, opened it, and pulled out a ten.

We watched him carefully, warily, wondering what he was up to.

He held out that ten toward me. "It was kind of you." He gestured with the bill. "Take this and get yourselves something to eat."

Tentatively, I reached out and took the money. "Thanks."

"Yeah, thanks," Ephraim echoed.

The cop shrugged and started to turn away. "Just one thing," he said as he turned back toward us.

"Yes, sir?"

"Don't come back, not to my park. We got enough drunks of our own."

"Yes, sir."

He jumped on that bike and rode away.

"Shit," Ephraim said.

"Yeah, shit."

CHAPTER 7 - TEQUILA

Chip was a sporadic regular at The Dew Drop; he'd show up almost every day for weeks and then not. He'd just disappear for a week or so. Then he'd start coming around again—looking bruised, dried out, and chagrined.

We always knew the reason: Tequila.

Give him beer or wine, vodka, gin, scotch, or bourbon, and Chip was as easygoing a drunk as you'd ever find. But let him near tequila, and there was going to be a fight. It wouldn't be his first shot or his second or even his third, but long about the fourth he'd start looking for somebody to take on. And he wouldn't give up until fists were flying. Luckily, or perhaps unluckily, Chip wasn't much of a fighter, so it was his face that usually got the worst of things.

Most times the brawl would get bad enough that the barkeep at whatever saloon Chip had stumbled into would call the cops. He'd end up in the drunk tank for a couple of days, then a couple more drying out at home, where he would be shaking and moaning and having the runs all the while swearing he'd never drink again – and then back to The Dew Drop just for a sociable beer or two.

There was one exception. One time Chip had nearly been locked up for assault. That was over at The Oasis. It was the same old story: Loaded on tequila, Chip goaded this guy until he slugged Chip in the face. Chip went down, and like he usually did, he got up and started with the fists again. The guy clocked him a second time. Same result. Third time, the guy started screaming. He'd broken his own hand.

The cops had tried to get this sparring partner to bring an assault complaint against Chip. The boys in blue don't like bar fights, so they wanted to teach Chip a lesson, which wouldn't have accomplished anything. Chip wasn't about to give up his tequila.

But the other fellow didn't want to do it. He must have figured everyone in town would be making fun of him. Of course everyone in town had already heard the story and were laughing anyway, so he ended up drifting away. I think his name was George something or other, but at The Dew Drop we still referred to the guy as Handy.

After a couple of fights early on, Sal had made a rule when it came to Chip: "Yous don't get no damn tequila in my bar!"

That didn't mean Chip never asked for it. Every now and again he'd forget or maybe hope Sal had forgotten and he'd order a shot. Sal would shoot him a look that would sink a battleship. "Not in my bar. Yous don't get no damn tequila in my bar."

Then Chip wouldn't show up for a few days, and we'd all know he'd gone someplace else to get his Mexican fix.

Of course, Sal couldn't be at The Dew Drop every moment. He hired part-time bartenders, most of whom were working their way through college and looking to make some decent money off the books. They usually didn't last long. The Dew Drop was a friendly enough place to work, but Sal was tight and the tips were pretty much nonexistent.

Magoo was one of those short-lived guys. We called him Magoo because he was nearsighted and wore thick round glasses like the cartoon character.

We liked Magoo for the one reason regulars at a bar like a part-time bartender: he was easy with the brew. Like he said, it wasn't his beer, it was Sal's. "And Sal ain't exactly what I'd call generous," he'd said the first time he'd swept up half-empty glasses and topped them off like he was serving water.

Strangely, much as we liked Magoo, none of us argued with him—not in the friendly way regulars use to give a part-time bartender a hard time. Some of us did, however, argue with Magoo that one night, the night Chip ordered tequila.

Ginny, who seldom talked and drank Long Island Iced Teas, said, "You're making a big mistake, Magoo. He can't handle tequila."

"That's right," Al had suddenly looked up. As always his fingers were snapping to a rhythm only he could hear. That day it is was a fast beat. And he was bopping his head around like it was listening to its own separate tempo.

A number of us added our chorused agreement, but Magoo ignored the warning. We knew what was coming, and he didn't. And come it did. Worse, I ended up in the middle. But it didn't start out that way. It started out with Chip going after Al.

"They suck," had been Chip's opening sally delivered right in Al's uninterested face. The words were accompanied by a plume of smoke from Chip's always-present cigarette.

"What the fuck?"

"The Cubs, worst damn team in baseball."

"Yeah, so?" Was Al the only person in The Dew Drop who didn't realize that he was wearing a Cubs shirt?

Was Chip the only person in The Dew Drop who didn't know that Al's clothes came exclusively from Saint Mary's—not the church, but the mission?

Wednesday was stew night at Saint Mary's. It was also the night the good sisters gave out clothes. Who could pass that up: stew and new clothes for the price of a sermon? Al had told us about it. Ephraim and I went regularly. None of us was Catholic, and I hated God, but the stew had chunks of real beef and there was usually a decent selection in the clothing room. So, what the hell, we went.

I'd been there earlier that day when Al had taken the shirt. "Al, I didn't know you're a Cubs fan?" I'd asked.

"I could care less. I don't think I've ever been to a baseball game, not even Little League. It fits good, and it's almost new. That's what counts."

"Yeah, I wonder how come it's here."

"Teenagers," Sister Bernadette said, "they change their allegiances almost as quickly as they outgrow their clothes."

I laughed. Al took another look in the mirror and said, "I'll take it, if that's okay, Sister."

"It will cost you two Hail Marys," she joked.

After dinner and some praying, when the three of us were leaving, Al wearing his new shirt, me carrying a grocery store plastic bag with a pair of jeans, Ephraim asked, "Did you ever go—?"

"To a baseball game?" I completed his question.

"Yeah."

"Yeah, once."

"I'll bet it was a Cubs game," Al joked.

"Actually, it was the Quad City Cubs and the Cedar Rapids Reds. I went with our church youth group. My parents always insisted that Jan and I, we hated it, but they were determined to make us good Christians.

"Everybody else was rooting for the Reds, so my sister and I, we screamed our heads off for the Cubs.

"I don't remember anything about the game, not even who won. I just remember there was this one kid; he was so pissed at us, at me. I loved it. If anyone ever asked me after, I'd say 'Cubs, they're my team.' It got so I almost meant it."

"How about you?" Al asked Ephraim.

"Never, nope. But I can sing *Take Me Out to the Ballgame*."

That was the song he was singing as Chip went on and on at Al.

"Don't be such a wimp."

"How come, jerk-off, how come the Cubs?"

"If you believe in something, you should damn-well stand up for it." That was the moment Chip got to me. It certainly wasn't the Cubs, or Al, or baseball. It was that he sounded so damn much like my father, font of judgment and truth. It was those shoulds and dos and don'ts.

"Who the fuck do you think you are?" I got in his face.

"I wasn't talking to you."

"Well, you're talking to me now."

He pushed; I pushed back. He swung; I connected with his nose, and blood started gushing. He made a grab for Jonny's pool cue, which set Jonny off. Nobody touched that cue. Jonny grabbed Chip just as I was swinging again.

My fist found solid flesh. Chip grunted, his head snapped back, then he slumped in Jonny's arms.

Jonny let go, and Chip fell to the floor, hitting the pool table on the way down. Chip's cigarette flew out of his mouth and toward the green felt. Jonny watched its flight with horror and then relief. He stomped on the butt and glared at me.

I looked down at Chip. Crap, I didn't know I could hit that hard.

Magoo grabbed a pitcher, filled it with water, and dumped it on Chip's head.

"What the fuck?" He got up fast, faster than I expected. Next thing I knew, I was down. That pitcher shattered all around me, and blood was flowing from a cut in my scalp.

I sat there stunned. Ephraim reached over the bar and got a towel for my head.

Meanwhile, Al and Magoo had taken hold of Chip and were pushing him towards the door.

Ginny, who was nursing her drink, said something that nobody could hear.

"What did you say?" Magoo asked.

"I said, 'He can't handle tequila.'"

"Now you tell me."

Chip was screaming, "Fuck you! Fuck you! Fuck you!"

Ginny gave Magoo the finger, "I did. You just didn't listen."

"She did," Al agreed.

"Tha's the truth," Sam said. He kept saying it over and over like it was a disconnected song lyric. "Tha's the truth, tha's the truth, tha's the truth."

"Whatever."

"Maybe you should go to the emergency room." Jonny was bending over me, his cue held like a lance in his left hand while he probed for shards with his right.

"Shit!" I yelled. "Ouch! Damn!" Each touch screamed pain.

"I'll take you," Ephraim offered.

"Nah, I think I'll just go home."

"It's gushing blood."

"It'll stop."

We discussed and argued for half an hour, by which time I was getting pretty lightheaded. In the end, I spent the night in the emergency room at City Hospital. A shot, stitches, something for the pain, and some blood.

Ephraim spent the night there, too, just hanging out and waiting for me, nodding off and startling up in one of those uncomfortable, chrome chairs, while I slept on a plastic covered gurney with a rock-hard pillow and soaked up somebody else's blood.

Chip didn't come by The Dew Drop for a few days. When he did show up, he looked a lot worse than I. "I told yous, no tequila," Sal proclaimed as Chip walked in.

"I know. I know. I'm sorry," he mumbled. "How's your head?"

Touching it gingerly. "It'll mend."

"Yeah, it always does."

I bought Chip a beer.

He bought me one.

Sal let Magoo go. He explained, "I had to. He was a nice enough guy, but he shouldn't have soived Chip no tequila."

"Yeah sure." Jonny sneered at Sal.

He had overheard Sal and Magoo going at it. Later he told us, "Sal wanted him to pay for the damages, and Magoo refused."

"Why should he pay for damages?"

"What damages?"

"A broken pitcher and a couple of towels."

"You're kidding."

"Sal wasn't. He wanted fifty bucks."

"Fifty bucks!"

"For a pitcher?"

"No wonder Magoo said no."

Ginny added her bit. "I told him he was making a big mistake."

"Yeah, you did."

She took another swig of her Iced Tea. "Tequila, it'll screw ya up every time."

Nobody told her. Sometimes what you don't know won't make a difference anyway.

CHAPTER 8 - BUDDHA'S BOITHDAY

The day had started well. I'd found a ten spot. I was washing out the garbage cans behind Chan's Delight, breathing in the wonderful aroma of rotting food and Clorox, and the money was just lying there, kind of plastered to the ground with muck and wasted Chinese. I washed it off, blotted it dry with some of Chan's paper towels, and stuffed it into my pocket.

Basic drunk logic: I figured it was a sign, quit early, and went by The Dew Drop to spend some of it—not all, just some.

I slapped the ten on the bar and told Sal to give me two bucks back. "For Iowa," I said and folded those ones into my hip pocket.

That's where I grew up, Cedar Rapids, Iowa. I was always talking about going back, visiting. I couldn't tell you why, but I was actually saving up—a buck here and a buck there stuffed into a manila envelope back of my socks and underwear.

Sal set me up. I felt good; I didn't usually get to run a tab—not even an eight buck one. It was great knowing I didn't have to fish around in my pockets looking for the price of my next drink.

"I don't get it," Tony said as he slammed his glass back on the bar for a refill.

"Easy," Sal cautioned; "them glasses don't grows on trees."

"Sorry, Sal, but what the hell's the matter with him? Iowa!" He gestured at me and shook his head. "His family don't want 'im, and I don't know why the devil he wants them."

"I don't want them, and I sure don't want them to want me. It's something else."

"Well, it ain't like you're going back to rub their noses in anything. If you'd made it, well maybe. But you." There was a sneer in Tony's voice.

He knew my story; all the regulars did. We all knew each other's stories. Over the years, one way or another we'd let stuff slip. It's easy to talk when you're drunk and easier still when you're with your buddies and they're drunk, too.

"Why does it bother you?" Ephraim asked in that mellow voice of his. "I don't want him to go 'cause he's my best friend and I don't want him

45

not being here, but you?"

Tony didn't answer. He gulped down his beer, thumped the glass down with a clunk, and lit out, slamming the door behind him. Sal stuck the dirty glass in the sink and cursed.

"I didn't mean to put a burr under his saddle."

"Yeah, I know. Something 'bout his own family I'd guess."

"Ain't it always," Chip butted in. "I don't know any of us have what you'd call 'family.' not real family."

"We were all whelped somewhere," Al always wanted to be part of the conversation.

"That's true, but bein' whelped ain't the same as belonging," Sal said. We were shocked into silence. Ephraim stopped his strumming, which usually meant he was taking a drink, but not this time. Sal seldom said anything, that is, besides "Yous want a drink?" and "Enjoys yourself." For him to actually say something was kind of disturbing.

Sal turned an exaggerated attention to washing glasses. He started clinking them together like it was the most important thing a guy could be doing.

"Sal?" I sort of asked.

"Yeah?"

"What you said?"

"Yeah?"

"I was wonderin'?"

"Yous was wonderin'?"

"Yeah," Chip cut in, "we was all wonderin'."

"Yous allowed." He kept on washing those glasses. I wondered how many times each glass was going to be washed before he'd stop.

"Every man's got his secrets," Al put in.

"But not in the neighborhood bar," Ephraim added. "So, Sal, where were you whelped?"

"Yous know what's my favorite holiday?" He dried his hands on a towel and started putting the glasses up on the drain board.

It was obvious that Ephraim's question was not going to be answered. "Christmas?" I guessed.

"Nah."

"Thanksgiving?" from Ephraim.

A shake of the head and a kind of queer smile.

"Easter?" Greg shouted from across the room. Who'd have thought he was even listening? He'd come in grumpy and unshaven earlier than usual and sat in the back corner, far from the action. It had seemed like he was just nursing his way to oblivion.

"No," Sal shouted back. It seemed he was enjoying the game.

"I know," Trish said.

"What?" I was getting that antsy, annoyed feeling I can get some times.

"Groundhog Day."

"Why would it be Groundhog Day?" I demanded.

"Because it don't count for nothin'. Just comes and goes and comes again, like us in this bar; we come and go and come back. Tony'll be back. Where else he got to go?"

There was no response from Sal.

"That's it, right, Sal?" Trish insisted.

"Close, but no cigar, Trish. Close but no cigar."

"Then what the fuck is it?" I was kind of glad that Chip was the one demanding an answer and not me.

"Buddha's boithday." He started wiping down the bar.

We didn't say anything—not at first.

Then the questions came. "When's that?" "Why that one?" and from Ephraim, "Who's Buddha?"

"That's kinda like Easter, ain't it?" Chip put in.

"Not really," Al responded.

Suddenly raising his head from the table where he usually sat indifferent to the rest of us, Sam started drumming on it and sing-songing "Buddha, Buddha, Buddha, Buddha."

"Hey, man, shut that up, will ya." I was getting more irritated and more uncomfortable.

"It don't matter," Sal said. "Now, all of yous shut up or I'm closing for the night."

"It's only seven o'clock," Trish protested.

"I don't care."

Just then Chuck came in. He liked to be called Charlie, but we all called him Chuck. "He looks like a Chuck," Al had said, and Chuck's name had been fixed.

Later on, somebody had asked what a Chuck looked like, and Al had laughed. "Like him," he had answered, and that had been true. Sandy-haired and light-skinned, Chuck looked like somebody who had once worked hard on his short, stocky body but had eventually let it go. The result was both a sense of muscular substance and flab, a confused sense that was intensified by the tattoo on his left arm near the shoulder. It was a dragon done in bright colors and breathing flame. Beneath it, and equally vivid, were three letters: M O M.

So Al and Tony took turns telling Chuck about Buddha. Chuck joked that Sal kind of looked like a Buddha and rubbed his own shirt-stretching stomach like it was some kind of joke.

And all the while, Ephraim was asking, "What's a Buddha?" "Who's a Buddha?" and "When's a Buddha birthday?"

Finally, Sal couldn't take it anymore, and he yelled, "Shut up, all of yous, just shut up. It don't matter so leave it alone or I swear I'm throwing you out."

We all shut up—again—for a while. All night the subject kept popping up like a Jack-in-the-Box in some kind of heat. Somebody would say something, and somebody else would say something, and pretty soon Sal would shout, and we'd shut up again, and again ...

When quitting time came for real and we were all leaving, I asked Sal, quiet like, "What is this thing about Buddha?"

"Since yous asking so polite and everything, I'll tell ya. It ain't nothin', not shit. I hate holidays 'cause I never had none. I never even had a real boithday, not my own, not for real."

"How c—?"

He cut me off with a wave. "That ain't important. Your life is like yous got a pot, nothin' in it. Yous puts in what you want and call it soup. Everybody makes his own. What's in it is what's in it, what ain't don't matter. Yous makes it and yous eats it.

"Some people thinks they can get it better by addin' what some other guy's got, tryin' to make their soup usin' somebody else's ingredients. Me, I know better.

"Nobody knows Buddha's boithday. The Buddha people they don't agree—not like Christmas or Ramaden, like those Japanese noodles."

I started to correct him, but he held up his hand again.

"See it don't matter. Nothin' matters. Ain't that the way? Just don't care and keep goin'. When it's over, yous'll know it. Know how?"

"No. How?"

"Yous'll be dead." He laughed a cynic's laugh, not with any funniness but not with any pain either.

I didn't say anything else; there wasn't anything more to say. I nodded. Let's go to Ephraim, and we headed out.

"So, when's Buddha's birthday?" he asked me half way back to Mrs. Buthyre's.

"Damned if I know."

"How do we celebrate?"

"We don't."

"We should."

"Why?"

"I don't know, for Sal, man. Doesn't he deserve a party or something?"

"Maybe," I answered, "but I don't think we're the ones can give it to him."

When we got back to our rooming house and said our 'nights, I pulled out that manila envelope, dumped the money into a heap on my bed, added the two bills from my hip pocket. I sat there counting what I had collected. A hundred. A hundred twenty, forty, fifty, fifty five, fifty six, sixty.

A hundred ninety-four sixty-eight.

Yeah, some day. Someday I'll have enough.

CHAPTER 9 - IN THE ARMY

"I served. I saw combat." That was as much as Captain would tell us.

Stiff and tall, it was hard to guess his age. "Old enough to know better," he'd told us, "but I've marched more miles than you might figure."

Had he really seen combat? He didn't talk about it.

Where had he been stationed? He never said.

What had been his rank? We didn't know that either. He was Captain because he was always inspecting and taking charge. "Too much foam on those beers," he'd announce when Sal wasn't careful to let the brew flow down the side of the glasses. "Rack those balls tighter," he'd instruct Jonny, who'd look up from the poll table and smile indifferently.

Captain would show up day after day for a time and then he'd disappear. "Where you been?" one of us might ask after a long absence.

"In the Army." Which made no sense until we understood that he was bouncing in and out of the V.A. Captain was one of those patients who won't stay on their meds. When he wasn't locked on the psych ward, he hung out at The Dew Drop.

No need to work, his benefits were enough. He apparently had and needed little. Yet, what he wore was always neat and carefully ironed.

Not needing a job didn't stop Captain from taking an active interest in the world of work. He'd stop to inspect and instruct wherever he could: pointing out smudges on windows and unpainted spots, stopping delivery men with instructions, "Those boxes should be arranged with the biggest on the bottom, not just jumbled like that." His pseudo-expertise knew no bounds.

He particularly enjoyed superintending landscapers. "Cut that back a little. You left some clippings. Some of these weeds need more spray."

One day, Riley, who was working a recycling truck, ran into him.

Captain was busily organizing a crew from Hanson's Nursery. They were working a condo community over on Foster, one of those that keep upgrading their grounds. The men, most of whom, probably not even understanding his English, good-naturedly ignored Captain. Their crew boss was doing what low-level managers often do: lying under a tree taking a nap.

The supervisor came by, saw Captain telling the men what to do, and the men working away. "You're doing a good job," he said and patted Captain on the back.

Captain saluted, which tickled the supervisor. He would have said more, but he noticed the crew boss sleeping. "What the hell?" he exploded.

Two minutes later the sleeper had been fired and Captain hired. "You stop by the office this afternoon and fill out the forms," the supervisor instructed.

Captain snapped to attention and again saluted, "Yes, sir."

"Yes, sir," the supervisor muttered as he took off for the next job site.

The men stood around staring at Captain. He stared back.

"Hey, Boss, what you want us do?" one of the workers asked.

Captain's eyes went vacant. He shrugged and wandered off. Couple days later he was back in the Army.

CHAPTER 10 - TALENT

About one thirty Tuesday and Friday afternoons, that's when the Black Orchid delivery truck would roll around to The Dew Drop. On it would be the kegs and bottles that kept The Dew Drop afloat.

Black Orchid had two drivers. Hunter, a young guy, fresh out of college and full of what he knew. His Uncle Hiram ran the distributorship; it belonged to Hiram's wife, who allowed her husband to manage things just as long as nothing interfered with her shopping or her travel. Hunter had great visions of rising in the company; selling more beer was his only topic of conversation.

"Sal, you aren't moving enough," he would complain.

"Yous sells what you can sells."

"What does that mean?"

"It means I got so many customers and they drinks so much beer. Maybe yous got to figure a way to get me more business." The bartender laughed and went back to wiping down the bar. It didn't need wiping, but Sal didn't enjoy Hunter's nagging visits.

The other driver, Sky, was a different matter. We all liked Sky. It was because Sky might be making the delivery on any given Tuesday or Friday that Ephraim and I always tried to be at The Dew Drop on those afternoons.

A full-blood Hopi, far from the reservation and happy to be, Sky loved his beer and his fellow human beings. The regulars at the Dew Drop loved Sky because of what he didn't love: work. "Work is an interruption of life," he had explained one day. "The Creator wants us live, not labor like ants."

Sky applied his philosophy by encouraging us to carry the kegs and bottles, full and empty, to and from the truck. In return, he stood us to beers, which he paid for with extra brew somehow mysteriously not requiring paperwork or accounting. We knew The Black Orchid Company would not be pleased by Sky's business technique, that old Hiram might call him a thief, but we also knew that if Hunter were the only representative of the distributorship, Sal might very well have looked elsewhere for his beer. Sky, with a thunderous voice rising deep in his barrel chest, always encased in a checked flannel-shirt, and his black felt hat banded by turquoise and sporting a feather dyed to look like an eagle's, was his own icon. Native American as stereotype: a piece of nature, history, and ambience. "How's the antelope running?" he would ask and then chuckle. "I forgot you boys only hunt elk.

"Help me drag some of these carcasses around," he'd joke and he'd make as if to drag an empty out to his truck. "And I have some live ones outside that need draggin' in." Immediately, he had all the willing hands he could want.

When all the hauling had been done, Sky would say, "The sun spoke to me this morning. There is much to celebrate. Let us show gratitude to The Great Spirit." With a nod and a wink, he'd reach across the bar and start grabbing glasses, which he'd hold under the taps and draw away.

"Hold on, Sky," Sal would bluster, "that's my job." He'd grab the glasses back and start filling them himself, knowing that there would be an extra half keg somehow materialized in the bar before Sky left.

There was one Tuesday that was rainy and kind of downtrodden. We'd gotten sopped on our way to The Dew Drop. I was shivering under my jacket, and I figured that Ephraim, who was only wearing a flannel shirt, must be miserable. Worse, the plastic garbage bag he was using to protect his guitar was slapping around in the wind making one of those irritating noises that can get a guy who hasn't had his first few drinks ready to jump.

"Shit, I could use a beer," Ephraim held the door of The Dew Drop open for me.

"Yeah. And a cup of coffee."

"You got something hot?" I yelled to Sal from the doorway.

"Close that damn door."

"Sure, sure." Ephraim pulled it tight behind us. "I need a drink."

"And coffee," I added.

"His coffee?" Sam laughed, the fingers of both hands snapping in syncopation. "No-nobody drinks that crap."

"Hey, watch yourself." Still, Sal had to half laugh at the truth.

"I'm desperate."

"You got to be." Still snapping, Sam slumped back so his head was resting on the tabletop.

"Hey, Sam, you want a cup?" I called, "I'm buying."

"Nah, I ain't ain't sle-sleepy. Ca-come to think on it, I ain't nev-never that that sleep-sleepy." He guffawed and lost his rhythms. "Damn! Just, just when I was get-gettin' it right."

"You sure were," Trish said. She turned to me and whispered, "Whatever the hell it is he's trying to get."

I chuckled and shrugged.

Sal snorted. "Yous actually buyin' yourself?" he asked Ephraim.

"Come on, Sal, we're miserable wet, don't give us a hard time." I dumped four bucks on the bar, enough for two drinks and two coffees.

My buddy was carefully unwrapping his instrument, checking to make sure no water had found its way into the case, slowly wiping it shiny dry with the remains of an old towel that was gray and tattered, but in his hands it turned to a sterile gauze wipe in the hands of a surgeon.

"I wish I had a woman who loved me as gentle as you love that guitar." Tony was sitting at a table drinking something that looked too good.

"What ya drinking?"

"Margarita."

"That's different."

"Yeah, I felt like something different."

"Well, just a regular for me."

"Regular it is." Sal put two shots and two glasses on the bar.

"And coffee."

"Yous'll get your coffee in a minute. I got to add some water to the pot."

"How long has that coffee been sitting there?" I hadn't noticed Ginny, sitting against the far wall and nursing her Long Island Iced Tea.

"Hey, Ginny. I don't think we want to know."

She laughed hollowly. "I don't think you want to drink it either."

"Probably not, but it's so damned cold." The word made me shiver again.

I took the two setups and carried them over to Ephraim, who was finally satisfied that his baby was dry. He took one of the shots in a swallow, picked up a glass of beer and half emptied it in another gulp. I was right with him.

"Yous want that coffee or not?" Sal demanded.

"Nah, we'll take another couple of beers."

"That's another forty cents."

"Yeah, I know."

"You're a cheap bastard, Sal." Tony was shaking his head. "If you can't give the boys fresh coffee, you should at least pick up half the price of that glass."

"Yous payin' the rent?" It was clear none of us were feeling very up.

"What time is it?" Chuck asked as he came in the door followed by a gust of cold, damp air.

"One thoidy," Sal answered. "Yous want a drink?"

"Yeah, sure." Chuck looked around. "He's not here yet?"

"Does he look here?" Tony asked.

"I hope it's Sky."

"Don't we all."

"Especially today."

"Yeah."

"Yeah, good day for drinking." Tony responded.

"Is there ever a bad day?" Chuck joked.

"Not that I've ever known," Ginny put in.

We sat there eying the clock and waiting for Sky.

"I got to piss."

"So go piss, you need Ephraim to hold it?" Chuck could be nasty.

"No. If he comes—"

"Don't worry, we'll call you."

"Yeah, don't worry."

"Okay?" I hesitated.

"Yeah, okay?"

"Okay." This time I got up.

Just then the door slammed open. Immediate disappointment. It was Hunter, dressed in raingear and looking as sour as the weather. "Got your delivery," he said in a voice that sounded like fingernails on a chalkboard.

"Yeah," I could hear the antagonism in Sal's voice. He didn't want to deal with Hunter any more than the rest of us wanted to do without that free beer.

I went to the bathroom door and stopped for a moment. "See you guys later." It was a stupid thing to say, meant only to give sound to our collective displeasure.

Ephraim took out his instrument and started strumming, looking for a song. "Hello, friend; it's me again," he started singing. I could hear his voice muffled through the door.

When I came out of the toilet, Hunter was wheeling a hand truck with a full keg across the room. He pushed past the bar into the storeroom. We could hear him muttering and clanging. Nobody had any inclination to help. He came back out with an empty. None of us even held the door. *Let him slip and slide. Hell, I wouldn't mind if he landed on his ass.* I laughed to myself at the thought.

The door opened, and Al splashed in. "Lousy out there," he commented, closing the door firmly; "the weather isn't particularly good either."

It took a second. We all chuckled just in time for Hunter to bang in again. It took him well over a half hour, hauling, banging, and muttering to himself about the weather. None of us offered a hand or even a word. When he had finished, he brought in his clipboard. There was a piece of plastic stuck over the papers, but they were still damp.

Hunter thrust the clipboard at Sal, who studied it carefully, said, "that much?" and signed. His pencil ripped the soggy paper. With a sigh he pulled a check out of his wallet, filled in the amount and handed it to Hunter, took the receipt and put that into his wallet before slipping it back into his hip. It was a slow-motion transaction that we had witnessed many times.

"You've got to sell more," the younger man insisted pocketing the check and rewrapping the clipboard in plastic.

"Yeah? Just how do I do that?"

"You need more people, more customers coming to The Dew Drop."

"Great, another brilliant observation. And how exactly do I do that?"

"You get in the paper, on the TV, on the radio. You get some publicity."

"I ain't got no money for advertising."

"The people who come to a place like this ain't gonna be listening to no ads anyways," Al whispered to me.

I took a slug of my drink and gave him a thumbs up.

"I'm not talking about advertising; I'm talking about being on the news. I'm talking about publicity."

"And just hows do I that? Yous full of great ideas, Hunter, but I ain't heard a how yet." I could feel the sneer in Sal's voice. "Just how do I get this publicity?"

"By winning." Hunter poked his finger at Sal's chest.

"Winning what? What are yous talking about?"

"I'm talking about a citywide softball league."

"A what?"

"A citywide softball league with teams from all the bars."

"Yer nuts."

"No I ain't." Hunter sat at the bar. "Got a cup of coffee?"

"For yous? Sure! It'll cost you forty cents."

Hunter fished in his pocket for some coins and dropped them on the bar. A few of us snickered, but nobody said anything. Sal set a mug on the bar.

Hunter took a sip. "What the fuck do you call this stuff?" he asked spitting the coffee back into the cup.

"I call it coffee. Now what are yous talkin' about?"

Hunter made a face that set Ephraim to laughing. I poked him, and he settled into a snicker.

"I'm talking about sponsoring a citywide league—all the bars Black Orchid supplies. It'll be fun and it'll get a shit load of coverage. If your bar wins, everybody will hear about it and they'll come in."

"Yeah, and if we lose?"

"It won't matter. It's not like you'll lose business. But I figure you're the kind of guy who'll like the challenge. Don't tell me you're going to chicken out on this." The guy had one of those smiles that make you want to clock him—a smile that says I'm smarter than you and there's nothing you can do about it. I was really hoping that Sal would tell him to take a hike.

"So what's it gonna cost me?"

"Nothing. Not a thing. We're going to cover everything, supply the equipment, the umpires, even beer for the players."

"How about the cheer leaders?" Ginny's question took everybody by surprise.

"What cheer leaders?" It seemed like Hunter and Sal asked the question simultaneously.

"You're not gonna have cheerleaders?"

"Who said we was even gonna …?" Sal sounded exasperated.

"I guess we could have them." Hunter smiled at Ginny hoping to win a little support. Of course he had most of us at the beer. If Black Orchid was providing free beer, we'd all be happy to play.

"What's in it for me?" Sal demanded. "These guys get free beer; what do I get?"

"I told you before: publicity. The bar that fields the winning team is going to get lots of free press. It's a real human interest story."

"Yeah sure, and the losers?"

"Sal, Sal, I never took you for a loser. Don't be such a pessimist. Look at these guys." He gestured to take us in. "Do they look like a bunch of losers to you? I don't think so. These guys are winners. Aren't you fellas?"

"Yeah, su-sure," Sam agreed. Ginny bobbed her head in agreement. The rest of us just sat there and smirked.

"So what do you say?" Hunter continued. "Are you going to let your best customers down?"

Sal looked at him and shrugged. "We'll see," he said in a tone he might use with a five-year-old.

"Just think of the trophy. A big trophy to go on that shelf." Hunter pointed to a shelf that was too high for bottles. It held a few fancy beer mugs, some old bowling trophy that Sal readily admitted had come with the place, and a china leprechaun with a bilious green hat. All of it was covered in dust. "It would give the place some class, some identity. People would come in and—"

"Sal," Ginny sang out, "that would really be nice." She gave him a big smile.

He smiled back and didn't seem to notice her missing teeth. "Yeah, I guess." He looked hard at Hunter, "Yous sure it won't cost me nothin'?"

"Positive."

"Nothin'?"

"I'm telling you."

"And the cheerleaders?"

"What about them?"

"Do we get free beer, too?"

"Yeah, I said 'yeah' before."

"Hey, Sal, you should do it. You really should." Ginny smiled at him.

"Who else is gonna be in this thing?"

"Almost all the places."

"Cochran in?"

"Yeah, The Oasis is going to have a team."

"Cochran agreed?"

"I just told you."

"Well, if that cheap bastard don't have no objection, I guess we're in, too."

This time we gave collective support with half-hearted gestures and shouts. Meanwhile, I was thinking, *Free beer. Hope they got plenty of it.* I was pretty sure the others were thinking the same thing. As for the softball, I could have cared.

A few days later, once all the regulars had heard and had made their comments, Chuck announced, "We got to get a team together."

"Who elected you boss?"

I was surprised by Tony's vehemence. *Why do you care?*

"Ya, y- you're r-right," Sam said. It wasn't clear if he was agreeing with Chuck or Tony.

Chuck backed off, "Nobody. Maybe we should start by electing a captain."

"Maybe it's up to Sal." Chip had come in with an extra buck and bought us all a couple of bowls of pretzels. That automatically gave him two votes even if there wasn't an election. We all munched a salty curlicue and nodded our heads in agreement.

"Hey, Sal," Chip used his momentary importance to get the barkeep's attention, "what do you think?"

"About what?"

Chip took a deep drag on his cigarette and blew the smoke towards the ceiling. A long ash hung precariously and then broke free to land on his chest before crumpling to the floor. A chain smoker, Chip's clothes were pocked with the burn holes of his carelessness. "About the softball league."

"Oh, that. I think Hunter lied. It's gonna cost me a bundle."

There was silence. None of us were prepared to discuss money, especially not with Sal.

"Turns out I gotta buy you bums uniforms."

"Just tee shirts," Ginny reminded him. "How much can that cost?" She smiled at him, and Sal half smiled and half scowled back.

Ephraim looked at her and at Sal, then he looked over at me and mouthed a question, "Is there something going on?"

I shrugged.

"Yeah, and yous wants a cheerleading outfit."

"Just for me and Trish and maybe a couple of the other girls if they want." She tried her damnedest to look cute. "Some of the others may want to play, but you wants cheerleaders."

"Why?" Chip had felt his momentary preeminence slipping away; he wasn't going to give it up that easily. "Why the hell do we want cheerleaders?"

"Not you, Sal. It's for the TV. If we're out there cheering, the cameras are gonna be on us, on our outfits with 'The Dew Drop Inne' plastered on the front. See that's what's gonna pay off. Right, Sal?"

"Yeah, sure," he answered in a tone that implied just the opposite.

Right, they're going to want pictures of you and the rest of our women? I wondered if the others were thinking the same thing. Of course, none of us were going to be rude enough to say it—not unless Chip hit the tequila. And then there was that free beer, which no one was going to oppose.

"Right, Sal!?" Ginny demanded this time.

"Yeah, right." He tried to make his answer stronger, more to her liking.

Ephraim shot me a look and again mouthed his question. I shrugged my response, "How the fuck do I know? Do I care?"

Chip tried again. "Anyways, Sal, do we start organizing or what?"

"Yeah, yeah. Yous do what yous do." Sal started washing glasses. When he got like that, we knew there wasn't going to be any more discussion.

"So what do you guys want to do?" Chuck was ready to move on. "Do we form a committee, elect a captain: what?"

This time Tony was more agreeable. "I think we need a captain."

"Yeah, who?" Sam downed a shot of vodka and picked up his beer. "Who who we got in this du-dump can be a cap-captain?"

"We need somebody can get us organized," Tony went on ignoring Sam's question.

"And somebody who knows how to play softball." My contribution.

"Good point," Ephraim added. "We need somebody who actually knows how to play the game."

"Like who?" Ginny wasn't through with her part. "I know cheerleading. Did you guys know I was a cheerleader in high school?"

"No fo-foolin'."

No one else responded. Nobody even sank to asking her how long ago that might have been.

"Tom." Chip blurted out the name.

"What? Who?"

"You guys remember Tom." He slurred the name out.

"Yeah. Su-sure." There were a few nodded heads and a couple of snickers.

"He was a great ball player."

"Really?" Chuck said.

"Seriously?" Al added.

"Then you'd have thought he'd know more about balls." Tony said. There was more snickering as we thought about Tom taking off with a transvestite. We hadn't seen him since. For all any of us knew he'd left town.

"Even if he was a great ball player, even if he was, what makes you think ..." Al was shaking his head.

"Yeah, and why would he want to help us?" This from Ray who looked like he was nursing a sick head and sounded like he had the flu. "You think he wants to come around here and have you guys laughing behind his back?"

"We can ask." Ginny suggested. "I can ask. Sharon and Trish and I. If we all go, maybe he'll feel—"

"Like we think he's a real man," Chip finished for her.

"A re-real man," Sam echoed.

"Yeah, like we think he's okay. Maybe that would make him want—" Ginny said.

"Fine, and where are you gonna find him?" Al put words to my own thoughts.

"The girls could go 'round to the other bars. He's got to be in one of them," Tony suggested.

"And if he is, and if they do, and if they ask him, why wouldn't that bar want him just as much as we do? How's that going to work?" I wondered if Chip wanted us to find Tom or not.

"I wouldn't come back here if I were him." The tone of Ray's voice was as negative as his words.

Just then Jonny came in. "Anybody want a game?" he asked as he went over to the pool table and started racking the balls.

"We was just discussing something."

"Yeah, we was just discussin' Tom." Chip came right to the point. "Weren't you the last one saw him?"

"Yeah. I guess."

"You know where he hangs out? We kind of want him for that softball thing."

Jonny looked at Chip for a while like he was lining up a difficult shot. Finally, "Yeah, I do. I run into him now and then still. He can't resist O'Grady's. We play a friendly game. He still ain't no good, but he keeps wanting to try me, and I feel kind of sorry for him. Anyway, I promised him I'd never tell you guys. I don't think he'll ever get over it." He rubbed his head for a moment like he had a bad itch or something. "Hell, if it had been me I might have left town altogether."

"So where does he drink now?" I asked.

"I don't think he does. He goes to meetin's over at the Luthan church on DeMott."

"They got a meeting over there?" Chuck asked.

"Yeah, it's kind of a nice one," Ray said. He was one of those guys who kept trying to quit and kept coming back to The Dew Drop— probably why he had so many of those lousy headaches. "Lots of rich women with too much time on their hands. You know the kind; they drink sherry while the kids are little. Kid goes to school, and mommy is downing martinis and banging the pool guy. By the time Junior's in high school she's got vodka hidden all over the house and the joy of herpes.

"Then they get religion. What they're really looking for is better lovers and a different drug."

A few of us laughed.

"And that's where Tom goes?" Al asked.

"Sure," Ray commented. "He's probably looking for women. Who doesn't love a woman who'll drink with you?"

"Do you think he'd come back? We could use him." Chip wasn't going to give up on that softball team.

"I got no idea. I just know he still plays at O'Grady's and he goes to that meeting. You want to ask him something, you go ask him."

"Yous want a drink?" Sal asked Jonny.

"Yeah, sure, gimme a beer." Sal put a glass on the bar. Jonny stepped over to put down his money and took the glass. He started to drop his change in Ephraim's bowl, changed his mind and put it in his own pocket.

"Cheap bastard," Ephraim mouthed to me.

Chip asked, "Who's going with me?"

"Where?"

"To that meetin'."

"Thursday evenin' ain't it, Jonny?"

"I don't know."

"Sure it is, Thursday."

"If you say so."

We mumbled about for a bit until it was agreed that three guys were going to go to the Lutheran Church meeting the next Thursday. Chip was one. Tony was the second; that was a natural because he had a car. They tried to get Jonny to go, but he refused, so I ended up number three.

My going had been Ginny's idea. "Tom likes Cal," she explained and everybody had kind of agreed. It wasn't something I wanted to do. I'd been to meetings before – plenty of them. They hadn't helped. They hadn't hurt, but they hadn't helped. You need a reason to stop, and I didn't have one.

***

The Lutheran church wasn't fancy, just classy in a low-key way. It wasn't on the street, but set back with grass and bushes, not just a parking lot. Most of the cars in the lot were washed and shiny—not like Tony's heap. Looking in their windows, the insides were clean, too. Maybe drunks drove them, but they were maintained by folks who knew how to keep up the veneer.

Inside, the church décor was simple and southwest. It seemed like deep red was the color of choice with just a few bits of turquoise and sky blue to accent. The doors were light oak, and most had frosted glass—no color or pictures. There were a few painting on the walls; they were of Indian pueblos and ceramics. The overall effect was halfway between a church and an airport. We were impressed and clearly out of place. Suddenly I was very aware of our clothes, our Goodwill specials— nothing fancy but trying to be appropriate.

"I don't think this is going to work," Tony whispered.

"Too late to turn back," Chip answered.

"Why not?" I was all in favor of running.

"We're here; we might as well do it."

"I guess." I was a reed in the wind.

We looked at Tony. "Yeah, what's the worst that can happen?"

I had visions of private cops coming out of nowhere, but I shrugged in my best know-nothing manner.

We followed a couple of well-dressed women through a door. "Can I help you?" one of them asked.

"Yeah, we were looking for the meeting." My mouth was dry cotton; what I really wanted was a drink.

The woman looked us over like we didn't belong, but she said, "Just follow us."

We were glad for the guides. The place had lots of classrooms and meeting rooms, each with a placard on the closed door; without them we could have tried twenty doors before we found The Parlor of Dismas.

"In there," one of the women said. As Tony pushed in, they continued down the corridor.

"Aren't you coming in?" Chip asked.

"I should say not," the other women answered, her eyebrows arched.

The door closed behind us. Suddenly we felt right at home. One meeting is just like another. The slogans pinned on a board, the coffee urn and Styrofoam cups on a battered table, the folding chairs in rows, and the people—most clumped and talking, a couple looking lost and not too steady, and a guy at the front getting ready to start us off. That guy was Tom, "Hi, my name is Tom, and I'm an alcoholic."

"Hi, Tom."

"Please find a chair so we can get started." Everyone slipped into the orderly rows of chairs.

"Let's start with the Serenity Prayer."

We stood and started by rote, "God, give me ..."

"This is bullshit." From the corner of my eye, I could see Chip shaking his head.

He's gonna go looking for tequila.

The meeting finally ended, and there was nothing I wanted more than a drink; nothing makes a guy thirstier than an A.A. meeting. I was glad we had a couple of sixes stowed in Tony's car. I figured they'd make the ride back to The Dew Drop a lot easier. And I figured the others were feeling the same way. But we forced ourselves to hang around and talk with Tom.

"I'm sober. It's been six months. I've got a good sponsor, I'm working on the fourth step, and I ain't going back to The Dew Drop or no place else."

"We're not askin' you to drink," Chip explained for the third time. "We just want you to play some ball." He went back over the whole trophy thing and how great it would be to win for Sal and for all of us.

"And you guys are my pals or something?"

"Yeah, we are. You're the one who left; we didn't do nothin'." Tom reddened at the truth of Tony's words. There had been no mention of Angelique, but the topic hung there like a piñata waiting to be hit with one of those softball bats.

I figured I'd add my two cents. "I think you've been pretty unfair to us."

"What does that mean?"

"So you were embarrassed. Big deal, we're your friends. Instead of letting us be there for you, you take off like we're making fun. How does that make us feel?"

"Like laughin' at me," half answer and half question.

"No! Like we'd let you down or something. I mean we felt shitty. Didn't we guys?"

Chip nodded. Tony said, "We sure did." I knew they both wanted to laugh as much as I did, but maybe we'd hook him yet.

"I didn't think of it that way."

"No foolin'. Well think of it now. We're your buddies and we could use some help. You don't have to do no drinkin'. It's great you're sober. That's terrific. It don't mean you can't play ball, does it?"

"I guess not."

"So think on it and help us out. Okay?"

"Yeah, I'll think about it."

"We're going to start getting the team together Saturday — around three. Be there, okay?" Chip asked.

"Like I said, I'll think about it."

We left, sure that Tom would be there on Saturday. By the time we reached Tony's car, we had plummeted into despair, equally sure that he would not and feeling that his involvement had become incredibly important. By the second beer, the entire topic had been replaced by a moment-to-moment reliving of Angelique's visit to The Dew Drop.

Saturday came around. Tom showed up at three fifteen. He'd already had a couple. "So much for sobriety," Jonny commented.

"Better to drink with friends than be sober with strangers," Tony added.

"I'll be damned," Ray observed.

I didn't say anything. To be honest, I didn't know how I felt.

Sal asked, "Yous want a drink?"

"Yeah, rye and a beer."

"Same as always."

"Yeah, I guess so."

"It's good to see yous."

"Good to see you, too, Sal." Tom sat down. It occurred to me that it was the same chair he'd always sat in. *I guess he's come home.*

Ephraim must have been thinking the same thing because he started singing *The Last Train Home.*

"Hey, can we get organized?" Ginny was taking charge.

Ray stared at her. "You've been getting pushy lately."

Ignoring Ray, Ginny said, "Ephraim, let's cut the music."

"Yeah, sure." He strummed a final chord and put his guitar in the case. "I was planning to start us off with *Take Me Out To The Ballgame*."

"Maybe later. Okay?" Tom stood up and mimed a batter's stance.

"Yeah, sure, Tom." My pal's voice sounded hurt, but nobody seemed to notice.

"So who's got some experience?"

Carol raised her hand. "I played in high school."

"No shit?"

"No shit. I pitched and caught."

"A double threat; but can you hit?"

"Three eighty good enough for you?"

"Damn."

"I thought you'd cheer with me." Ginny sounded miffed.

"Not if I can play."

"I'll cheer." Sharon's offer kind of threw us.

"Great." Ginny sounded halfway between enthusiastic and upset.

"Anybody else got experience?" Tom was taking his role seriously.

"Some," Chip offered.

"Yeah, me, too," from Chuck.

"If you count phys ed," I said.

Tom nodded.

"Well, in that case," a couple of the other guys added.

Al made a show of flexing his muscles. "I can't do much in the field, but I can hit well enough."

In the end only Ephraim and Sam hadn't said anything. "Sam, you?"

"C-count me out, I d-don't p-play. Maybe maybe I ca-can help the g-girls with the cheering. I got got the rhyth-rhythm." He drummed on the table to prove his point.

"That's a plan," Al said. Then he whispered loud enough for everybody to hear, "Too damn hopped up to do nothin'."

Sam lifted his head as if to object and then let it settle back to the table as if to agree with Al.

"See what I mean?"

"Leave the guy alone," Trish hissed.

"Yeah, sure." Al looked at Ephraim. "What about you?"

"I've never played, not even in school. I've seen them play baseball on television, but I don't know the rules or nothin'."

"I guess we got our manager," Chuck offered. There was a chorus of agreement. Enough business, it was time for drinking. Ephraim got his guitar out, and Saturday was in full flow.

The next week the team shirts and hats came in, and we were all pretty psyched—especially Ginny who had chosen the colors and the lettering. She and Trish had even gone shopping for some shorty-short skirts, which Sal had surprisingly bought. The four cheerleaders—Sharon and Bev rounded out the squad—looked ridiculous. We all told them they looked great and that none of the other bars would have anything like them.

It turned out they had even gotten together and worked up a couple of cheers. Bev's daughter was cheering for her high school, and she had helped them learn the routines. Nobody laughed or made comments, but later Ephraim asked me if we weren't all making jerks of ourselves.

"Yep. Who cares? We'll have fun … and free beer. I mean what the hell."

"Yeah, I guess." He didn't sound convinced.

"Anyway, you're the manager. You won't be making a fool of yourself no matter what happens."

"Yeah, I guess." This time there was more energy in his voice. "When do you guys actually start practicing?"

"Damned if I know. Maybe we should ask Tom."

It was a couple more weeks before we had a few of cheap softballs and bats. Hunter had come through with some flimsy catcher's gear, but there were no gloves for the fielders. Sal cursed Hunter as a cheap piece of crap.

"That guys on my list," Ray told us.

"What list is that?"

"People I wouldn't mind killing off."

We stared at him.

"He may not be at the top, but the son-of-a-bitch is on it."

Eventually, Sal found a deal on some used gloves, which would do. "I'd like to take it out of Hunter's hide," was his only comment when we thanked him.

"Remember that guy Cody?" Al asked. We all nodded in assent. "That hat he wore?"

"Yeah." "Sure." "What about it?"

"Hunter kind of reminds me—"

"Of Cody?" I didn't see the connection.

"Hell no! Of that sidewinder."

We practiced in the park, trying to clear the broken glass out of the way. We used pieces of cardboard for bases, and duct tape to keep those cheap softballs from falling apart.

We may have been acting like kids, but we certainly didn't have childhood devotion to the sport. Most of the time we showed up for practice well into our daily drunk. After an hour or less, we'd head back to The Dew Drop for refreshment and rehashing of every dropped ball, missed catch, and wild pitch.

There wasn't as much fun in discussing the good catches and the powerful drives. Besides, they were few and far between.

There were, however, some positive surprises. Carol was as good as she claimed. She and Tom took over as our permanent battery—switching between pitching and catching as their tired muscles demanded. Chuck actually could hit, well enough that we had to limit him for fear that he'd destroy our practice balls. Sal was already fumed over the costs, and he wasn't about to replace anything.

Then there were the clowns, those of us who were falling all over ourselves. I was one of the worst, which was no surprise. I had been one of the worst in junior high gym class, and I certainly hadn't improved with age.

As manager, Ephraim took care of the equipment, which was kept in the storeroom at The Dew Drop. One day he borrowed a couple of gloves and a ball and asked if I'd like to teach him how to catch and throw.

"Sure, why not. We'll go to the park tomorrow morning." I promised feeling like I was a big brother.

It didn't take long for the tables to turn. He was a natural. Even hung over, my pal could handle grounders, flies, long drives. And that arm of his! After a couple of sessions in the park, he could have passed for a real player. I suggested we try hitting.

"Sure, if you think I can."

"Yeah, I think you can."

The problem was for hitting practice we'd need a couple of more guys, especially somebody who could pitch. After the next team practice, while we were sitting around at The Dew Drop, I mentioned that Ephraim would like to try hitting. "Maybe a few of us could get to the park early Wednesday," I suggested.

"Sure," Tom answered; his voice didn't sound very convinced.

"I'll pitch for you," Carol offered. "I can get off work a little early."

"Let's do it," Tony said as he pounded back a beer. It wasn't clear if he was talking about softball or some crazy drunk scheme.

"Yeah, let's do it," Chuck echoed, which really scared me.

They were all there—eager like kids and raring to go. Chuck seemed subtly changed, talking quietly with Ephraim, answering questions, and patiently demonstrating over and over again. I couldn't hear them, not from the outfield. Everybody else, all ranged around the infield, had laughed when Tom had waved me out there. "Just in case," he had shouted.

It was just as well; that way I couldn't make a fool of myself trying to field some lucky bloop off Ephraim's bat. "No problem."

It was a Little League field with a low fence that marked homerun territory. Litter had blown against the fencing. I absently pulled some flyers and newsprint free and let them sail in the breeze that was blowing from home plate. I was a kid again, back in Cedar Rapids, not interested in what was important to other kids, but also not sure that I was interested in anything else.

From the corner of my eye, I saw Carol start to pitch. It was a slow, looping pitch that perhaps even I could have hit. Ephraim lunged and, off-balance, swung his bat in the air. Chip started to say something. Chuck cut him off and moved close to Ephraim, whispered something in his ear, and backed away. "Another one," he called.

Carol obliged. It was another creampuff.

I wasn't really paying attention, but I still heard the solid thunk of aluminum against ball. "Wow," somebody shouted as the ball sailed over the infield, over my head, over that Little League fence.

I stood there for a minute in our whole team's amazement. Then as I headed for the fence to climb it and retrieve that ball, I heard Ephraim yelling, "Hey, that's fun."

"Pitch to him this time," Tom had yelled at Carol, "a real pitch."

My back was to the action. I was bending to retrieve the first ball when a second flew past and landed a good thirty yards beyond. Holy crap.

Everyone was screaming. I turned back to see Ephraim dancing his way around the bases. Chuck was jumping up and down. Tom's arms were in the air. And Carol was slouched in disbelief.

It was pretty clear who was going to play and who was going to be the new manager. And that was fine with me.

"I'm sorry, man," Ephraim said as he helped me carry the motley equipment back to The Dew Drop.

"No problem. I guess we found you another talent."

"Yeah, I suppose." He paused for a moment. "You know, I wonder?"

"Yeah."

"I mean do you think?"

"What might have been?"

"Yeah. I mean if I'd started playing—"

"As a kid," I finished for him.

"Yeah."

I laughed. "The Cubs well maybe, but The Yankees, nah, never."

He laughed, too, but I don't know if he got the joke. I'm not sure I got it either.

CHAPTER 11 - PROMISES

It wasn't often that Ephraim and I ate breakfast. If we did, it was a cup of coffee and a roll from the Quickie Mart. If Herb was on duty, he'd throw on some butter for free. Otherwise, we'd grab a couple of packets of ketchup and mayo. That would do it.

But there were those special days when we'd head to the hole where Carol waitressed. *Gabbys 24—7* blinked in orange neon out front. It was a lie. Gabby opened at five to catch the going-to-work trade and closed at midnight, after the A.A. groups had drunk their last cups of coffee and smoked their last cigarettes. On Sundays, he opened late, eight o'clock. During all those hours, Gabby was there, sitting at the register and yelling at his waitresses. Kansas, his main cook, didn't get yelled at. It would have been difficult, maybe impossible, to find another grill-man. So when Kansas ticked him off, which was often enough, Gabby would take it out on those waitresses and occasionally on the customers.

Gabby didn't care for us customers, especially the regulars from The Dew Drop. He knew that we only showed up when Carol was working and only sat at her station. He figured that she'd give us extra refills on the coffee and maybe an extra side. And she did, too, even though we didn't tip. Family don't tip, and we figured we were family.

Every once in a great while, when we were feeling extra flush, maybe to celebrate a birthday or just to feel good, Ephraim and I would get up earlier than usual and head down to Gabby's for some pancakes. That was Kansas's best thing, pancakes like nowhere else. It didn't hurt that Carol would slip some bacon and sausage on the plates, even though we didn't pay for it.

I loved those pancakes. I'd never had pancakes before I met Ephraim. We didn't have them at home. "Such things are frivolous," my father would say. "Frivolous was another word for ungodly and sinful. My mother obediently made us Cream-of-Wheat, which Jan and I choked down with resignation.

I hadn't understood what made pancakes "frivolous" until I ate some of Kansas's. Even then, it wasn't the pancakes that got to me; it was the maple syrup. That was something!

"It's not real, you know." Ephraim told me the first time.

"It sure tastes good."

"You ought to try the real stuff, the stuff from maple trees. You gather the sap and boil it down. Boy is that good."

"Let me guess, your mother made it."

"No, actually that was my father. We traded some in town, but we used it, too. Better than sugar."

"I'd like to try that, but this will do for now." I poured even more of the sticky amber fluid on my plate and slurped away.

Carol brought around more coffee. She had a few strips of bacon wrapped in a napkin. Trying to look nonchalant or absentminded, she left the napkin on the green-gray Formica table.

"Stop catering to those bums and take care of the real customers," Gabby growled.

"Sure thing, boss," Carol responded. As she walked away, she gave us a quick smile. "Use lots of that syrup. It kills the skinflint."

I did as she asked.

"You know we can come back. You don't have to eat it all today."

"Yeah, I know." In my guts I didn't believe it. I shoveled dripping forkfuls of pancake, bacon, butter, and syrup into my mouth and followed them with swigs of sweet black coffee. I drifted back to Cedar Rapids.

Tim Grader was a member of the church, which made him an acceptable employer for a high school kid with summer vacation ahead and a father who didn't believe in "frivolous."

"A summer farming won't hurt you," my father had told me. "It might even toughen you up. You can live at the Grader's and come to church with them." Not what I wanted to hear, and not how I wanted to spend my summer.

There was one saving grace. At the end of the summer, the Graders were going to Washington. "Tell you what, Calvin. If you work out, I mean really work out, we'll take you along," had been the offer.

For a kid who'd never been out of the state, the thought of a trip to the nation's capitol was pretty tempting; that it would be without my parents made it seem like a gift from heaven.

"Thanks, Mr. Grader. You won't regret it."

Farm work didn't agree with me. Sleeping in the hayloft didn't either. It wasn't the sneezing, bad as that was, but the feeling I was one of the animals. I tried to live with it. I got some pictures: the Capitol, the Washington Monument, the Lincoln Memorial, even the White House. I had them taped up over my bed, so each morning I'd be reminded of the trip that was coming.

"You ready, Calvin?" Mrs. Grader asked me on that great morning.

"Yes Ma'am." I threw my suitcase into the back of the pickup and climbed into the bed.

"You might be more comfortable riding in the cab," she said sweetly.

"I'll be fine up here, least for now." I snuggled down against the cab and pulled my sweatshirt tight. "Ready," I yelled to Mr. Grader as he got behind the wheel.

Soon we were on the highway, the miles humming under the tires.

We sped down the road, and I, tucked into my corner, recited the Gettysburg Address and Lincoln's Second Inaugural into the wind. Excited by the prospect of the trip, I had made it my goal to memorize them.

With malice toward none; with charity for all; with firmness in the right, as God gives us to see the right, let us strive on to finish the work we are in; to bind up the nation's wounds; to care for him who shall have borne the battle, and for his widow, and his orphan — to do all which may achieve and cherish a just, and a lasting peace, among ourselves, and with all nations.

I spit the words into the wind, in my mind watching them flow over a country in the midst of war. *Ain't this grand?* I started reciting again.

We didn't turn on I-80. *What the devil?* I wanted to pound on the cab, get his attention and find out what was going on, but I knew better. *He'd probably just light into me. Maybe he's still testing to see if they should take me along.* I went back to my reciting. Hunkered in the truck bed, I closed my eyes against the wind and settled in. *Maybe I'll fall asleep.*

I woke up as Grader pulled the truck onto a dirt road. He stopped next to a poplar. "Come on, Cal, jump down and say howdy to people.

I knew some of the folks; some I didn't. "Where are we?" I demanded.

"Washington. I told you we were going, and we have."

"This isn't Washington." I said feeling stupid.

"Sure it is. Washington, Iowa, best camp meeting the church puts on."

Jan had laughed at me when I got home. "You busted your hump for nothing, Cal," she said and danced around the room.

As irritated as I was, I couldn't help laughing along with her. "At least I learned something."

"What would that be?"

"In this life a promise don't give nothin'."

"Cal!" It was the third time that Ephraim had called my name. I'd been lost in my memory. "Carol gave me the bill. We should get going. Gabby will be on her ass if we stay any longer."

"Yeah, sure." I finished off the last drops of my coffee and took the bill from my friend's hand. "That was a great breakfast."

"Yeah, and the way Carol totaled the check's not bad either."

I took a look. "Free bacon and lots of refills, the way breakfast …"

We walked to the register. Gabby stuck out his hand for the slightly blued paper. "How many slices of bacon did she slip you boys?" he demanded.

"Four," I answered suddenly uncomfortable.

"Four each? Is that what you meant?"

I nodded assent. He added the bacon to the bottom of the bill. "If that woman had more friends like you two no-accounts, I'd have to fire her.

"As it is, I'm not going to charge for the extra coffee. You know you only get one refill."

I gulped and handed him the money.

"Carol," he called as he rang up the sale and counted back my change, "next time this guy wants pancakes you bring him a bottle of syrup that's near empty. I can't afford customers like him."

"What do you think about that?" Ephraim asked as we headed out.

I didn't say anything, I just remembered, *In this life a promise don't give nothin'.*

CHAPTER 12 - BUDDHA, BUDDHA, BUDDHA

"What's going on?" Greg and Ray were standing outside The Dew Drop taking turns unsuccessfully trying to get into the front door. It was well past opening. The night grates were open, but the shade in the front window was still down, the open sign wasn't on, and most importantly, the door was locked.

"Have you knocked?" Tony asked. He, Ephraim, and I had met up at the corner—by the Laundromat across from the Bodega where Chuck cleaned up and where he sold pot to the local kids.

"Of course we have," Greg answered. To prove his point, he pounded on the door. He put his ear to the door. "I think there's somebody in there."

"Is it Sal?"

"How the hell would I know?" He pounded some more.

Ephraim walked away from the little group. "Where you going?" I asked.

"Thought I'd try the back door."

"I'll go with you," Ray offered. They started for the alley.

"Damn," Ray yelled.

"What is it?" I called to them.

"Nothing," Ephraim called back.

"A God-damned rat, biggest fucker you've ever seen," Ray shouted, "nearly bit me."

"Is the door open?"

"We're not there yet."

"I hear somebody," Greg announced. He pounded again.

Sal's muffled voice, "I'm coming. Hold your water." The lock turned. "What's the matter with yous guys?"

"The door was locked."

"Yeah, so." Sal looked different, a bit happier but also like he wasn't quite put together, maybe messier than usual.

"Where were you?"

"In the back. I was woikin' on the books. I figured I'd take myself a few minutes."

None of us believed him, not with business waiting out front. No one said a thing, we just filed in.

Right behind us, Ephraim and Ray came in. Ginny, looking very sheepish was with them; Ray held her right arm. "She was coming out the back door just when we got there," Ephraim reported.

"Yeah, trying to straighten her hair as she walked," Ray added.

Ginny, her face red, was trying to arrange her clothes with little bumps, grinds and pulls. She was wearing what looked to be a new dress—something prettier than her usual, a bright yellow hair bow, and a necklace of turquoise beads and red coral.

"You and Sal doing some serious cheerleading?" Tony asked.

"Gimme a drink," Greg demanded. "Leave it alone. It ain't none of our business," he added to the room.

"What da ya mean it ain't our business?" Tony challenged him.

"What ain't whose business?" Trish asked as she walked in the door.

"Ginny and Sal—" Ephraim started.

Trish cut him off. "That ain't any of our business." She went over to Ginny, patted at her back and pulled a few wrinkles smooth. "You look nice," she half whispered.

Ginny didn't respond. She pulled free of Ray, who was still holding her arm. "Where ya goin"?" he asked.

"I gotta use the toilet." She blushed even more furiously.

Meanwhile, Sal had said nothing. He poured Greg's drink, put it on the bar, and took the money Greg had put down. Greg stood there staring. When Sal didn't speak, Greg demanded, "Where's my change?"

"What? Oh." Almost furtively, he pulled money from his pocket and handed it over with not even a "sorry about that." He glared around the room defying us to say something. "Yous want a drink or what?" he insisted as if nothing was going on.

"Good for you," Tony said and reached across the bar to pat Sal on the shoulder. I chorused his comment and smiled in Sal's direction.

The barkeep pulled away. "Yous want a drink or don't you?"

"Yeah, gimme a drink."

The rest of us started ordering. Trish went over and knocked gently on the bathroom door. "Need any help in there?" she asked quietly.

Ginny cracked the door open. A few moments later we could hear the two women laughing.

Ephraim took out his guitar and tuned it.

I downed my shot, took a swig of beer and helped myself to a couple of pretzels.

"Ya know what today is?" Ephraim asked me.

"Thursday," I answered.

"Yeah, sure, but that ain't it."

"No?"

"Nope. It's Buddha's Boithday," he said trying to imitate Sal's voice. He laughed. I laughed, too. Pretty soon we were all laughing—even Sal. Only Greg wasn't laughing; he sat scowling across the room. Oh, yeah, and Sam was nodding off on his table. For once even his fingers had stopped; he was totally gone.

The two women exited the john. Sal nodded, asked Trish if there was something she wanted. She ordered a beer. He gave her one and put another in front of Ginny.

Ginny smiled at him. "Thanks, Sal," she said in a honeyed voice. With her left hand, she gently touched that turquoise necklace and smiled.

He smiled back.

Greg got up, carried his now empty glass to the bar and put it down with a little push that sent it spinning. "I think I'll go over to The Oasis," he announced.

Ginny started to say something and seemed to think the better of it. She just shook her head.

"What's gotten into him?" Ray asked.

"God, men can be stupid," Trish commented.

Ephraim strummed a loud chord. "Hey, Sal," he said, "Buddha, Buddha, Buddha."

CHAPTER 13 - PRANK

"S-sky, you're one of one of the Ho-hoppy Indians, ain-ain't you?"

"Hoppy and happy," Sky responded as he did an impromptu dance.

"That's Hopi," Greg corrected.

"Don't matter," Sky said.

"S-sorry," Sam responded at the same moment.

"Don't matter," Sky repeated. "Good for a laugh." He danced a little more.

"The r-reason I was askin' is you I-indians got lots of s-secrets: ma-magic and s-stuff."

"I got secret to make you do my work—glass of beer." Sky guffawed. "That good secret."

The rest of us laughed along with him, but not Sam. He was dead serious. "Ca-can you s-see the future?"

"Everyone see the future," Sky managed to get the words out in the middle of his laughing. "Next week, I come back with more beer. You all here. Jonny play pool. Ephraim have guitar. Cal is with him. You see, future easy."

"I think he had something more in mind," Greg said.

"I know. Sam want solution for problems. Most white men ask Indian for solution. They think money solve everything, Right, Sam?"

Sam bobbed his head in embarrassed agreement.

"You want way to make much money?"

Another head bob.

"You ask Indian how to make money. Now that funny." Sky laughed again. "Maybe beads, but no money."

Once more, we laughed along with him.

"I j-just th-thought," Sam stammered.

"How about I cast Indian spell and get you lottery ticket."

"The w-winning t-ticket?"

"No guarantee winning ticket, but who knows. I do Indian magic for you. You give me dollar and I buy ticket."

Sam searched in his pockets and pulled out a pile of change. Carefully he counted a dollar's worth. "Here," he held out the coins.

Sky took it, and he, too, counted it carefully. Then he put it in his breast pocket. "Special money. I use these for ticket."

"O-okay."

"What do I get if you win?"

"Half the the m-money."

"No good, I can't benefit or magic won't work."

"W-what do you w-want?"

"You buy all my friends a drink. Everybody here, all the regulars at Dew Drop."

Sam nodded agreement.

***

A couple days later we were surprised. Sky came into The Dew Drop not to make a delivery but to wave a lottery ticket in front of Sam. Sam reached for it, but Sky said, "I have to hold until drawing. I come back Friday to deliver. Bring ticket so you can cash."

Sam nodded. The rest of us were nodding, too. "What do you think?" Ephraim asked me.

"I think the chances are somewhere between slim and none."

"Me, too. But Sky seems kind of confident."

"I guess."

The others were buzzing, too. As the conversation continued, the excitement and conviction that Sky had bought a winning ticket grew.

Sam was most sure of all. "I I'm going to go go home and sh-show them," he stammered. "They s-said I'd never am-mount to n-nothing."

"Well, don't forget our drinks," Greg reminded him.

"A a pr-promise is a a promise."

"Yous all gonna be here Friday?" Sal asked.

"We wouldn't miss it," Chuck announced.

"No way," I agreed.

"Whose gonna bring the numbers?" Greg asked.

"W-what numbers?" Sam asked.

"The winning numbers so yous can check the ticket. Yous want to know if you won or not, don't you?

"I'll bring the paper," Jonny announced.

That made it official. This was a big event, even Jonny was getting involved.

***

Friday came, and we were all there. Jonny had brought the paper, and it had been passed around until we'd all memorized those winning numbers. When Sky arrived, it was spread in front of Sam, who was drumming away on the table. While Sam drummed most of the time, that day the rhythm seemed especially manic.

"Yous on something?" Sal demanded.

"No. W-what would would make y-you ...?"

Sal shook his head and went back to wiping down the bar. "Nothing," he mumbled.

Ephraim was picking away at his guitar. He sang as he picked.

> I feel lucky, I feel lucky, yeah
>
> No Professor Doom gonna stand in my way
>
> Mmmmm, I feel lucky today

It may have been the first day of April, but the wind was blowing and biting. When Sky came in dragging his hand truck loaded with a keg of Miller, a gust followed him into The Dew Drop. The newspaper threatened to scatter. Chip, who was sitting opposite Sam, slammed his hand down. The sound startled Ephraim; his usually careful fingering gave way to a discordant twang. Jonny missed an easy shot and yelled, "Damn!"

"Boys seem a touch uptight," Sky said. "Some of you want to help with these kegs?" he added.

Nobody moved or responded. Finally, Sam demanded, "Did did you br-bring it?"

"What are you talking about?" There wasn't a hint of a smile or any other indication that Sky knew what we were all thinking about.

"My t-ticket. The w-winning ticket. Did-did you bring it."

"Oh, yeah, your ticket. I don't know if it won anything, but I have it here." He reached into his breast pocket, pulled out a piece of paper, and handed it to Sam. Sam read the numbers off while Chip checked them against the paper.

"Five," Chip announced. "You got five of them numbers. You didn't win it all, but you sure got a fistful."

Sam was drumming on the table in delight.

"Holy shit." "You did it," "Sky, you're something else." We were all excited.

Sky watched us celebrate. When Greg clapped him on the back, he smiled back and said nothing.

"So when are yous buying those drinks?" Sal asked.

"When when I get the m-money. I got to c-cash in this this ticket."

"Let's go do it," Chuck announced. "Let's go get you that money."

There was a chorus of agreement.

That's when Sky started to laugh. "April Fools, you guys. April Fools."

"What does that mean?"

"It means that ain't the ticket for last night. I bought it this morning and put in those numbers to fool you guys."

"You suckered us," Jonny said.

"Guess it was my turn to do the hustling, Jonny."

"Damn," Jonny turned his attention back to the table. "You damn Indian," he muttered.

"Got you guys good," Sky chuckled. "You really think Indian can do magic. Boy, that's good."

Sam sat dejected and angry. "Fuck fuck you, S-Sky."

"Where your sense of humor?" the deliveryman asked. "It good joke?"

"F-fuck you," Sam responded.

"Who help bring in beer?"

A few of us set to work. At least we'd get some free beer.

Sky was getting ready to leave, when Sam asked. "So where where's my t-ticket."

"What ticket."

"The one you sh-showed us the other d-day. The one you you s-said you b-bought."

Sky fished around in his pocket and found the weary piece of paper. "You want it? Here you take it." He handed it over.

Sam looked at it for a minute. "H-holy sh-shit," he announced.

"What?"

Chuck took the ticket and looked, too. "You got three of the numbers. It won't be a lot, but you'll have enough to buy us all a drink."

"What what are you t-talking about?"

"That's what you said," I reminded Sam. "You said you'd buy us all a drink."

"That's what yous said," Sal confirmed.

"Damn, and I never looked," said Sky. "I just wanted to do joke."

"No shit." Jonny bent over the pool table. Click, click, click: balls hit one another. One thunked into a pocket and ran down the gutter.

Ephraim started a new song.

CHAPTER 14 - BLOOD MONEY

I was scrubbing the stove at Chan's when we heard the news. Chan liked the sound of voices, so the news was always on. I would have preferred music, some of that nice twangy Country or the blues to match my mood. But the cleanup guy doesn't get much of a vote.

Even with the vent fans going full tilt, the fumes from the degreaser were getting to me. It was a job I hated, but the boss wanted it done. My eyes were smarting and my nose running.

Chan, a cigarette dangling from his mouth, was watching me. His work over for the day, the old guy wanted to go home as much as I wanted to get to The Dew Drop, but sometimes things have to be done.

"Pileup on I-40. At least thirty-eight vehicles including a Greyhound Bus involved. Dozens injured, some seriously."

A moment later the keen of an ambulance ripped the quiet. "Bad accident," Chan said.

"Sounds like." I took the opportunity to step away from the fumes.

"Where you going?"

"Just going to duck out the door and get a breath of fresh air. Can I borrow a cigarette?"

"You borrow, you no pay back. I know that. I give you one." Chan knew I had my own pack, but he also knew that his Marlboros were way better than my Broncos. Normally he told me to smoke my own, but when the work was really nasty… I appreciated the thought.

It was late enough for the streets to be quiet. In the distance I could hear the sirens: fire and police along with the ambulances.

"More cars in pile," Chan announced when I had finished my smoke. "Other side of road, too. Bad mess." The singsong of his voice hid any emotion. I wondered if he cared or was simply amused. "They need blood. Ask donors come to hospital."

"You going to give?"

"They no take my blood."

"Why not."

"It Chinese."

"That's dumb," I said. "I've heard of blood types like A and B and positive and negative, but Chinese blood. That makes no sense."

Chan was laughing.

"You were joking."

"Lazy bones, enough cigarette. Get back to work." Chan picked up a cleaver he used on ribs and waved it towards me. It was another part of our ritual, his dumb way of saying that I was okay.

I pulled the rubber gloves back on and went to work. *The sooner I get this done, the sooner I can get a drink.*

The radio was blaring on about the accident. Details seemed to flash into staccato headlines.

A green Chevy van had blown a tire. Someone had estimated its speed at ninety plus. No wonder it had flipped.

Seven known dead.

A coyote and eight illegals or maybe just a poor Mexican family. We can't be sure.

The city blood banks are overwhelmed.

All emergency personnel are ordered to report to their superiors.

The governor has called out the guard.

The governor has asked all tow truck drivers to help. The state will pay.

Chan sat, cleaver still in his hand, listening. I finished the stove and announced, "Chan, I've had enough. I'm gonna get sick if I have to use any more of this shit."

"Okay, Cal, you go have drink. I know you need." He laughed that inscrutable laugh of his like he had me all figured out. He was right, of course. He paid me, and the money made the nausea a lot more tolerable.

"Maybe you go sell blood; make more money?" he added.

I didn't answer.

"They pay for pint. Just like sell wonton soup."

"Yeah, but I don't do that. I work for skinflints like you. I don't have to sell my blood."

"Then maybe you give blood."

"Maybe you'll go give some, too."

This time Chan didn't make a dumb joke. "I think I will. I close and go to hospital."

"Well, you got me pegged, I'm off to The Dew Drop."

"They need blood. Even Chinese blood they need."

I laughed. "Yeah, even Chinese."

The Dew Drop was quiet when I got there. Sal was wiping down the bar with a dirty bar towel. With nothing going on, he looked sad and out of place.

"Where is everybody?" I asked.

"Giving blood." Trish answered. "If I could, I would've given too, but they don't want my blood."

"Oh."

"I g-gave the other day, so I can't, n-not today," Sam stammered. He did a slapping drum roll on the table before he lost interest and seemed to loll back into a half-sleep.

Sure. Not if they did a drug screen.

Ginny and Ephraim came in. "You guys give blood?" I asked.

"Yeah. They're payin' fifteen a pint tonight." Ephraim answered. "I said 'what the heck and let 'em take a pint. What about you?"

Before I could answer, Sal angrily asked Ginny, "Yous were selling your blood?"

"No, not me, him." She pointed at my friend. "I just gave it to them. Those people needed it, and I got plenty." I could see the wink she gave Ephraim. That was fifteen bucks Sal didn't need to know about.

A few minutes later Al came in. "Yous been selling blood, too?"

"What are you talkin' about? I was over at the Maxi. Shelly and I were splitting a bottle of Gallo and takin' in the new flick."

"So yous ain't hoid?"

"Heard what?"

"About the pileup on the highway." I supplied.

"No shit?"

"Real bad. They've been asking for blood."

"You give?"

"No, I was at Chan's working. Maybe after I have a drink or two. Want to go with me? They're paying good."

"Yeah, maybe." He gestured to Sal for a drink. "You think there were any Mexicans involved?"

"Yeah." Ephraim answered. "They're saying the first car, van, was full of them. Why?"

"I don't want to give none of my blood to no Mexicans. You give them American blood and they'll think they're as good as us."

"Al, that's downright dumb," Tony said. He'd come in during the conversation. "Blood's blood. Mexican, American, even Indian, it's all the same red. When you're in the hospital and you need it, do you ask who gave it? It—"

"Yeah, I do," Al cut him off. "It ain't all the same. I knew a guy once, nice guy. He got hurt, cut off his arm. Feeding one of those wood chippers and damned if he didn't stick his arm all the way in.

"They gave him lots of blood. Some of it must have been from a nigger or something 'cause he went bad after that. Started stealing. Ended up in jail." He paused. "If it weren't that blood, what was it?"

"I think I'll go give that blood now," I announced.

"You selling it, Cal?" Ephraim asked.

"No, I think I'd rather just give it. There may be a Mexican kid down there who can't afford fifteen bucks."

"Think I'll go along with you. Maybe I can give the money back." Ephraim stood up.

"Yeah, you guys do that." I saw Ginny furtively put her fifteen dollars into Ephraim's hand. "Give them that money back," she said. "Ain't that right, Sal?"

CHAPTER 15 - PEARLS BEFORE COPS

"There's no way!" Jonny looked up from the felt covered table and nearly dropped his cue. "There is just no way."

"Yeah, and he's been there for five days already."

"Shit."

"Yeah. It sucks."

We nodded. It wasn't that we knew Riley as well as Greg did. Even when he was at The Dew Drop, Riley didn't talk about himself.

Greg had come by The Dew Drop first. An easy-going guy, he had fit in just fine. Soft-spoken and polite, he told a few jokes and stayed out of politics. Drank rye and beer like most of us, and slipped Ephraim his change. Never showed off or bragged. Just a regular guy. It was only after he brought Riley around that we learned he was educated, a teacher. He taught auto repairs at the high school—not fulltime, but still he taught.

How Greg and Riley had met, how they had become friends—that we had never learned. One thing was sure, Riley wasn't educated. He certainly wasn't a teacher. He was a scruffy guy who spent most nights at the Biltmore Hotel, that SRO on Front, the one just down the street from Saint Mary's Mission. Some nights he didn't have money for a room so he slept at the bus station, or the city shelter, or just on a park bench.

Anyway, Greg brought Riley around one afternoon and bought him a drink. There was a little grumbling, mostly from Al, because Riley was a black guy, and most everybody who hung out at The Dew Drop was white. Of course, we had an occasional Mexican drop in, but they weren't part of the regular crowd. They'd sit in a corner and drink and yammer away in Mexican till they'd notice Sal was ignoring them and maybe that their drinks were kind of watered-down.

So Riley was something different. Maybe Al's grumbling about Negroes and how they never knew when they weren't wanted would have discouraged Greg from bringing him around again, but it turned out that Riley could sing. I mean that guy really showed Ephraim up, which didn't upset my pal at all. Pretty soon the two of them were doing duets and laughing like they were buddies, and that meant Riley was going to be a regular no matter what Al or anyone else might have thought.

A big guy, Riley always wore a black overcoat and a dark green watch cap. If you had met him on a dark street, he would have looked really menacing. But we all knew he was an easygoing guy, quick to laugh—loud and hard, and quicker to share whatever he had.

Even though we didn't know much about Riley, he had slowly become one of us. Tom had even asked him if he wanted to play softball. As the season approached, everyone was getting excited about The Dew Drop team. But not Riley. "I'm more of a lover than an athlete," he said with a booming, infectious laugh. "I just like to play in bed."

Most of us dismissed it as brag. Besides, what did it matter? Riley's comment did push Al's buttons. "I just don't want to think about no nig…, no Black guy makin' love," he announced with venom.

"None of our business what Riley does or doesn't do," Chuck responded, "'specially if he ain't doin' it in here."

Al muttered a bit and stormed out. "I never noticed before," Chip said.

"What?" I asked.

"Al's tats, the one on his left hand.

"Yeah, a few dots, what about them?"

"They're jail tats."

"So?" Ephraim asked.

"Aryan Brotherhood. The guy's a Nazi."

"Wow."

"Yeah."

Eventually Al came back. Life went on. Life at The Dew Drop went on the way it was supposed to. There were two big differences: we had the infectious laughter and resonant voice of Riley to buoy our spirits, and most of us were just a little uncomfortable when Al was around.

One afternoon Greg came in. "Riley's in jail," he announced in a somber voice. "They say he's the Box Cutter Bandit." He had a copy of the morning paper. On the front page was a picture of Riley handcuffed and being dragged around by two detectives. Scowling guys named Brown and Swanson, the two cops were in charge of the case and taking all the credit they could for having captured this dangerous criminal.

That was when Jonny had made his pronouncement and we had all nodded in stunned agreement. There was no way that easygoing, likable Riley had been holding up women, stealing their purses and jewelry, and slashing their dresses with a box cutter. It just didn't seem possible.

"Somebody ought to go down there and talk to him, find out what's going on." My suggestion met with instant agreement.

But who was to go? It had to be somebody the cops would let in, somebody who wasn't so afraid of the police that they'd end up tongue-tied. Which left me out.

"You for starts," said Greg. "It's your idea."

"I don't do cops," I half stammered.

Sam, for no reason, sat up and commented, "I I d-don't nei-neither. F-f-forget that."

"Nobody asked you," Tony sneered at him. "Damn hophead," he added more quietly.

"I ain't n-no …" Sam, slouched his head back onto the table.

Chuck shook his head almost painfully. "Sal, we ought to do something. Why do you let him — ?"

"The guy comes in, pays for his drinks and he don't hurt nobody. Most of the time he don't even say nothin'. What he does to himself, that ain't none of my business. Ain't none of yours neither. It ain't like I need the table."

Ephraim laughed. It wasn't a real laugh, more shallow, like it hurt.

"Who's gonna take care of Riley?" Jonny reminded us.

"How about Greg?" Ephraim suggested, which made good sense.

"Yeah, and Sal," Tony added; "he's a businessman. They have to let him in."

"And Sharon; there should be a woman." We all agreed with Chip even though nobody could have told you why.

"I ain't closin' for the afternoon, not for Riley or none of yous guys,"

For some reason, we all felt it was important for Sal to go so we argued and wheedled until he agreed to call one of his backups. The thing that convinced him was Tony talking about the softball team and how Riley being in jail could really hurt The Dew Drop. "I can see that Monica broad doing a story now. "'Specially if we win the trophy. What'll she headline it? A bar for athletes and perverts? Yeah, that'll do

The Dew Drop a lot of good. Sal, you want publicity or publicity?"

Trish said she'd go around to Sharon's place and get her to join the expedition. After she left, Greg said, "Shit, I forgot. I got to teach this afternoon."

"No, you got to go down to the jail. He's your friend."

There was more arguing and discussing until Greg finally asked Sal if he could use the phone. "Twenty-five cents," Sal demanded.

Greg started to reach into his pocket when Chip stopped him. "Sal, are you serious. The guy is giving up a day's pay, and you want a quarter to use the phone? Are you really that cheap?"

It seemed to me that Sal wanted to say yeah he was, but he didn't. "Yeah, okay. For this yous can call free," he pronounced as if he were making a major concession. He put the phone on the bar, and Greg called the school to tell them he was sick.

He was a damned good actor, making his voice sound hoarse and faking a couple of sneezes. "Yeah, I'm sure I can make it for the next class." A pause. "No, I'm going to spend the day in bed." Another pause. "Yeah, Cheryl, I know lots of liquids." Then. "Yeah, thanks. You take care, too." He hung up and smiled at us. "Maybe I should teach drama instead of auto mechanics."

We laughed.

"Maybe it would have been better if you were a lawyer."

The laughter stopped; we knew Chip was right. We all looked around like we didn't know what to say or do.

"He must have someone from Legal Aid," Tony commented.

"Lot of good that will do him." Jake said shaking his head in a hangdog way. "Legal Aid lawyers don't do nothin' but make plea bargains." He downed his shot and took a big swallow of beer. "I should know."

Yeah, you should. Jake had just finished eight months in lockup and swore he was innocent.

This time the laughter was really uncomfortable. Chip started to tell the story about his own run-in with the law.

Jonny cut him off, "You've told us…" He let his voice trail off.

"How many times?" I added.

After a moment, Chip said, "Yeah, I know; I just wanted to—"

"It don't change none with the tellin'," Greg said.

"Where the devil is Trish?" Greg asked. "I thought she was getting Sharon."

"It takes a while. A lady has to get dressed for the occasion."

Chip stared at me. I knew he wasn't one of my fans, but sometimes he could get downright nasty. "Since when is Sharon a lady?" he asked.

"She's the closest thing we have to one around here," Greg replied.

"Hey, there's nothing wrong with any of the goils," Sal put in.

"You mean like Ginny?" Ephraim took the opportunity.

"Yeah, yous got something to say?"

Ephraim shook his head. No sense in getting into an argument—especially not with Sal.

We sat around drinking and waiting. I poked Ephraim and pointed at his guitar. He shook his head. I poked him again. Reluctantly he picked up his instrument and started strumming. The song was *Jail House Blues*, which seemed to fit. He sounded mournful as he sang:

> I don't mind bein' in jail, but I got to stay there so long, so long,
> I don't mind bein' in jail, but I got to stay there so long, so long,
> When every friend I have is done shook hands and gone.

"I guess we all felt like crying. Maybe my idea hadn't been such a good one after all.

Eventually Trish came back. Sharon was with her. So was Ginny. She immediately went over and kissed Sal, who came out of the embrace with a big shit-eating grin.

"Ginny, you going down to the jail with them?" I asked.

"Sure, if Sal wants me to."

"Nah, it ain't no place for you." We all smirked and tried to hide our smiles from Sal. Everyone knew that Ginny had spent her share of time in lockup.

"Whatever you say."

"So when are you guys going?" Chip was impatient.

"As soon as Harry gets here." Harry was the latest in Sal's string of relief bartenders. He wasn't particularly well liked. The guy was almost as stingy with the brew as his boss; and he was even stingier with the pretzels, not that they mattered so much.

Harry took his time getting to The Dew Drop. "I had to finish a paper and drop it off at my professor's office," he explained. Did we believe him? Did it matter? We were all impatient and the drinking we had been doing made us even more so.

"Let's get going," Greg almost ordered Sal and Sharon.

"Yous take care of the joint,"

"Sure, Sal," Harry responded.

They got ready to leave. I don't know about the others, but I was thinking I needed another drink. Sitting around and worrying makes me thirsty as hell.

It took a lot of drinks before they returned.

They were a rather downcast group. Chuck, who had come in during their absence, commented, "You guys look like they already hung him."

"Hanged," Al corrected. We looked at him like it really mattered. "Sorry," he muttered.

"It sucks," Greg announced, turning to Harry, who was getting ready to leave, "A double and a beer, man, before I start breakin' stuff."

The bartender looked at Sal, who nodded assent, and poured Greg's drinks. "You want me to stay?" he asked.

"Nah, won't do any good. I'll woik it..." Sal sidled back of the bar, pulled some cash out of his pocket and paid Harry. "I know it's gonna fuck up my image, but I give ya an extra ten since yous came in when yous wasn't supposed to."

"Thanks, man." Harry seemed almost as surprised as the rest of us.

"So," I asked, "what the hell's going on?"

"They got him dead-to-rights," Sharon said. She slumped into a chair. "God, I need a drink."

"There's no way," Greg responded. "It just can't —"

"He fits the description."

"Sure, but there are lots of big black guys around."

"Lots?" Tony wasn't buying that.

"Well, maybe not lots, but Riley isn't the only one." Clearly Greg was still on Riley's side.

"And the box cutter. They found a box cutter in his room."

"Of course he'd got a box cutter." It surprised me that Al would speak in Riley's behalf. "He works at Recycle The Planet, part of his job is cutting up boxes and tying up the cardboard."

"They'll say the recycle people have cutters for him to use."

"Maybe, but it's still something reasonable for him…" Most of us nodded.

"And the poils?" Sal asked.

"What?" from Ephraim.

"Pearls," Sharon explained. "The cops say they found a string of pearls in his room."

"What the devil would he be doing with pearls?"

"Maybe he forgot them when he was sellin' the rest." Chip sounded like his faith was slipping.

"You don't believe that, do you?"

"Who knows?"

Greg scratched at his armpit and scowled. "I know Riley, and there's no way."

"Does he got a lawyer?" Ginny asked.

"Yeah, some Legal Aid kid. You remember his name, Sharon?" Sal asked.

"Sawyer," Greg answered for her. "Anyone know him?" We all shook our heads.

"They come and go so fast," Tony pointed out.

"It don't make no difference," from Jake.

"Then there's the biggest problem," Sharon said. She took a drink of her rum and coke.

What some people drink. Out loud I asked, "What does that mean? There's more? What the hell's the biggest problem?"

"It means …" She took another sip. "It means that whoever was doing those robberies has stopped, which makes Riley look guilty. Like, if he's innocent, how come there haven't been any stickups in five nights?"

Yeah," Chip put in, "whoever it was they was doing it almost every night before this."

"That's true," Chuck added to no point.

"I got to use the can," Sharon said. She walked to the bathroom and opened the door. Just before she went in, she turned back to the room. "I hate to say it, but it don't look good for Riley."

She was right, and we all knew there weren't going to be many good citizens in Albuquerque who'd care about a big, black, drunk going to jail for a long time. What they wanted, cared about, needed, was a sense of security. If the robberies had stopped and somebody was in custody, they'd be just fine with it. What we thought wasn't going to matter. Maybe that was what hurt the most—especially for Greg. It was a tossup whether he was going to start crying or just throwing stuff.

"Maybe he'll start again," Ephraim suggested.

"Or show up in another city like that sidewinder Cody," I added.

"Maybe," Greg grunted, but it was clear he wasn't expecting any miracles.

Sharon banged out of the bathroom. "I got an idea," she shouted.

"What's that?"

"Carol's brother."

"What about him?"

"He's a cop, right?"

"Yeah, so what?" I asked.

"If he'd put in a word for Riley ..."

"What good would that do?"

"Why would he?" Greg and Chip spoke at the same time.

"Then maybe they'd actually take a look at it," Trish said. "Isn't that what you meant, Sharon?"

"Exactly." Sharon looked so pleased with herself that nobody wanted to point out that all the evidence seemed to point to our friend. Besides, there was still Chip's question—why would Carol's brother put himself on the line for Riley? Riley wasn't even around when that Cody business went down. I kept my doubts to myself. At least there was something to hang on to, and Sharon again believed in Riley's innocence.

Sal promised to talk with Carol, and the rest of us promised to keep thinking of ways to help, which meant we'd have a good reason to do a lot of drinking. I had to work at Chan's. His regular evening dishwasher had gone to Cheyenne for his brother's wedding, and that meant some good money for me—as long as I could force myself to scrape those filthy plates and keep from vomiting. Of course it also meant giving up some evenings at The Dew Drop, but money was essential, and I needed it to drink. After all, Sal wasn't giving that beer or booze away.

It wasn't until the weekend that anything important happened. The Box Cutter Bandit must have been listening to me; he showed up in another city, Santa Fe. Obviously it couldn't have been Riley; he was still stuck in jail.

Of course the cops and the D.A. didn't necessarily see it that way. Riley wasn't released. Greg went down to Legal Aid on Monday. I went with him. We asked for Mr. Sawyer, and this squirrelly looking guy called us into a little cubical he shared with somebody who wasn't there. The three of us were crowded in.

The lawyer's squeaky voice and acne-pocked appearance did nothing to give us confidence. Greg started right at him. "How come my buddy's still in jail?" he demanded.

It might have helped if he'd mentioned Riley's name first. Sawyer got defensive before he even knew that we were talking about Riley. I tried to step-in. "Our buddy Riley was charged with those box cutter holdups," I explained. "Now the guy's up in Santa Fe, which means Riley didn't do it."

"Oh, yeah, that colored guy."

I wanted to smack the guy. I could see that Greg, too, was ready to go after him. "How about it?" I asked hoping for some kind of positive response.

"I hadn't heard anything about Santa Fe," was what I got.

I had the newspaper under my arm, and I stuck it under Sawyer's nose. "Right here," I said jabbing my finger at the story. *I wish Sal were here to say something. Maybe this goon would listen.*

Sawyer took a moment to read the story and another to think about his answer. "Well, that doesn't prove he's innocent," he finally commented. "This may be another guy, a second perpetrator." He said the word carefully, pronouncing each syllable distinctly.

Greg slapped himself in the forehead. "Yeah, another big Black guy using a box cutter and going after women who are alone." He shook his head in disgust. "And cutting their dresses." Another shake. "Obviously two different men."

"You're joking, right?" Greg's voice dripped with contempt.

"There are copycats you know."

"You don't think maybe you should go and ask a judge?"

"Ask a judge what?"

"To let Riley out of jail," I suggested not too helpfully.

There was a long pause. "There's evidence, you do know that, right?"

"He always had a box cutter for his work," I tried to explain.

"It's the pearls that are the problem," Sawyer opined. "He certainly doesn't have any call to have a pearl necklace."

" It's an S.R.O.," Greg pointed out. "Who knows who stayed in that room the night before or the night before that?"

"Actually, your friend had been in there for four nights running, and before that was another guy. So it's kind of likely that that necklace was from your buddy, and why would he have a pearl necklace lying around? Can you explain that to me?"

He had us there, which pissed me off. "Have you seen the necklace?" I asked, because I couldn't think of anything else to say.

When he didn't answer, I pressed him. "Is it even one of the things that was stolen?"

Slowly, without feeling, he answered, "I really don't know. I just figured—"

"You just figured it must be the big black guy," Greg finished for him.

"No." The lawyer was getting red with anger or embarrassment, who could tell which? "I figured the cops would have checked it, I mean, you know, they have the lists and everything." He was beginning to stammer, not a good sign in an attorney.

"Well, maybe with this other guy, maybe you should check out that necklace and see if it's on their list." I had pushed forward until we were nose to nose. Somehow it was Chip all over again except Sawyer backed off. Since there wasn't much room in that cubicle, he was pushed against a bookcase and trying to learn back into those law books.

Greg put his hand on my shoulder. "Hey, let the guy breathe."

I stepped back.

"Thanks." Sawyer was obviously feeling intimidated.

"So you'll check it out?" The anger hadn't faded out of my voice, but I was back in control.

"Yeah, sure."

"Today!" Greg held his hand up forefinger extended to make his point.

"Yeah, sure, today."

Sawyer was true to his word. Riley came bouncing into The Dew

Drop that very afternoon. Most of us were there—except Sharon, she had to get to work. The rest of us had been ragging on Sal because he hadn't gone with us to the lawyer. Somehow we figured it was his job.

"Yous guys need me there for moral support?" He was trying to sound tough.

"Yeah, sure," Greg was all over him.

"You was intimated?" Al asked. "Those cops intimate you?"

I could see Greg getting ready to correct him.

That's when Riley came in with the biggest shit-eating grin I'd ever seen. He shook everybody's hand like it was some sort of ritual; it almost felt like we were in church. He even shook with Al, who nodded his head in some kind of recognition like there was something between them— something that wouldn't ever be said out loud.

The cops had refused to give the big man back his box cutter, but he had that necklace in his coat pocket. He pulled it out, and we could all see it nestled in his big, black, callused hand. Anybody could see it was just costume junk.

"That was their evidence," Chuck said. "It's god-damn crap. Who'd steal shit like that?"

"A dumb cop," Tony commented, and we all chuckled.

"I gotta give it back to Gladys," Riley said.

"Gladys?"

"Yeah, you know the hooker who works on Gold and Amo."

"The one with the green hair?" Jonny asked.

"Yeah, she's the one."

"Why that color? I don't get it."

"It makes her stand out. Guy drives by, sees her under a streetlight, he notices." Greg answered before Riley could react.

"I never thought of that."

"Maybe I should dye my hair—maybe something bright orange."

I wondered if Ephraim was serious.

Chip whistled long and low. "Wow, she's kind of young."

"Kind of?" Al echoed.

"You were with her?" Jonny asked sounding surprised.

"Sure. And she ain't so young."

"Nah, she's a pro," Al winked, "a real pro."

"Shut your mouth." Riley growled.

"How much she charge you?" Al asked; he was never one to leave it alone.

"Nothin'. She and me, we share a bottle of Thunderbird and have a good time."

"Let those g-good times r-roll," Sam croaked from his usual slump.

"Carlton ain't gonna like that," Al commented. I could visualize the angry pimp who dominated the girls who worked Main. Carlton was a major player and one mean son-of-a-bitch. We all knew he carried a gun and didn't mind using it. "He could really fuck you up."

"It ain't none of his business. She does me after hours."

"Still." I couldn't keep the note of discomfort out of my voice.

"Still what, boy?"

"He's not exactly one to share…" My voice trailed off.

"Well, that box cutter of mine does have its uses. I'd never hurt no lady or rob no one, but Carlton come around my room or he hurt Gladys for bein' with me, that's another damn story."

"Yous want a drink?"

"Course I do. Seems like I've been in jail for years."

We laughed, perhaps a bit nervously. Chip and Tony clapped Riley on the back. Ephraim strummed a loud chord.

"Can yous pay?"

"It's on me," said Greg. He put a five on the bar and slung his arm around his pal's shoulder. He couldn't quite reach, but it was close enough—and that was enough.

Riley had his drink and went off to find Gladys. He came back an hour later. "They ain't hers," he announced.

"What are you talking about?" Jonny wanted to know.

"Them pearls, they ain't hers. Gladys says they ain't hers, that she'd never wear no crap like them." He held the necklace up like it was show and tell.

"So how did they get into your room?"

"I don't know. I figured she'd dropped … Who the hell …?"

We sat around doing our best thinking. Beer followed rye, and rye followed beer. "I bet it was him," Tony announced.

"Who?"

"Carlton. I bet he learnt about you and Gladys and set you up." There was instant agreement from most of the room.

"You sure of that?" Jonny asked.

"Why you askin'?" Riley demanded. "You know something we don't?"

"I know Carlton ain't the only one who'd get pissed about you and Gladys."

"You thinkin' of Al?" Trish put in.

"No fuckin' way," Chip insisted. "He may be a prick, a prejudiced prick at that, but settin' somebody up with the cops ... I don't believe it."

"What don't you believe?" It was Al just banging in the door.

"You know something about these pearls?" Riley demanded.

Al looked at them really carefully. He held out his hand and Riley dropped them into Al's outstretched hand. He looked at them some more. "Cheap shit," he pronounced.

"Yeah, we know that," I said. "Did you put them in Riley's room?"

"Who said that?" He demanded. "Who the fuck says I'd do something like that? Was it you?" Suddenly he was nose to nose with me. I could smell the sourness of his breath.

"Somebody planted those pearls," I said. "Tell him Sal."

"Whoa, I ain't takin' no sides here. We's all friends, and yous all customers. Enough!"

Grumbling, we let it go.

A couple of days later, Greg and I suggested to Riley that maybe we should go talk with Sawyer. "How come?" he asked.

"'Cause somebody told the cops about you. How else would they have gone lookin' at you? It's not like you've got a record or anything. Somebody had to drop a dime."

"You think so?"

"Absolutely."

"But how would Sawyer know?"

"He's looked at the file. He was your lawyer. He should know."

Sawyer didn't know. At least that was what he said. "They don't tell me anything that isn't part of the case," he explained. "A source, a confidential informant, an anonymous tip; who knows—they don't tell us,"

We never learned how those pearls got into Riley's room. We never knew how the cops had known to look.

Maybe like so many things, perhaps it just didn't matter; nothing much changed—except Riley, he changed. He didn't sing—kind of pushed Ephraim off. He didn't laugh—not in that boom-box voice— and he didn't see Gladys, not anymore.

He and Greg continued to hang out at The Dew Drop, but Al kind of disappeared. Maybe he left town; none of us saw him around. Tom asked Riley to take Al's spot on the softball team, but he said no, which put me back on the roster to everybody's consternation.

After a while, nobody mentioned Al—except once in a while Ephraim would sing those Jail House Blues, and we'd wonder, just for a moment, we'd wonder.

CHAPTER 16 - SHADY REST

Sunday nights I worked at The O'Rourke Shady Rest Home. It seemed like a better name for a cemetery than a nursing home, but the patients didn't appear to notice. Actually, when I was there, they didn't seem to notice much; they were asleep. I worked from eleven until five doing what had become my basic task in life, cleaning.

At The Shady Rest I cleaned bathrooms. I don't know if they were cleaned other nights, but on Sundays it was my job. I would start at room seventeen and worked my way back to one. Then I'd go upstairs and start again—thirty-four to eighteen. By that last room, morning would be starting to stir. Nurse and aides would scurry about handing out pills and taking count of who had and had not survived the night. With their arrival, I would try to become as inconspicuous as possible, finish up, and disappear for another week.

Those bathrooms were dirty and smelled. It was an unpleasant job, but Mr. O'Rourke paid well. He must have liked my work because he asked on a few occasions if I'd come in a second night a week to do the kitchen and dining room. I would have taken that on, too, but those nights he wanted me to work seven till one, which would have meant no Dew Drop.

I didn't have much interaction with the residents, which is what they called the patients. Once in a while one would wake up while I was in a room. Usually, it was to use the toilet, so I'd get out of the way and leave them to it or, if they needed help, I'd go get one of the aides who hung out in the lounge watching television and napping. Then, of course, there were the few times when one of those old folks would wake up, see me, and start screaming. They must have figured I was Death come to clean them out of this world or maybe some robber going to take the few cents worth of belonging they had left.

Mostly, the residents just slept right through. That made sense since they were given sleeping pills every night. Some of them might talk or whimper or even cry in their sleep, but they seldom woke up to see me mopping and scrubbing, which may have given them something to watch.

There was one exception, Morty Jones. Mr. Jones was in room twenty-two. When I came into his room my first night working at The Shady Rest, he pointed to his roommate. "That's Jim. He talks a lot and don't make no sense."

I laughed and went on cleaning. "Shouldn't you be asleep?"

"I don't take their damn pills. I'm not ready, so I'm saving them up."

"Ready? For what?"

"To go home. When I want to go home, then I'll take their pills. Not until."

"Oh," I said not really understanding him.

"What do they call you?" he asked.

"Cal, and you?"

"In the old days most people called me Mr. Jones. My friends called me Morty. Here they call me 'the old fool in twenty-two,' or the 'difficult one.' Yeah, I hear them call me that."

"Well, if it's alright with you, I'll go with Mr. Jones."

We chatted as I finished the bathroom.

"You do a good job, Calvin."

I blushed, not so much from the compliment as being called Calvin. We said goodnight, and I hurried on to room twenty-one.

Week after week Morty Jones and I had a conversation. It wouldn't be about much, but he talked away until I had to move on to the next room.

He didn't like to talk about his health. "My liver's gone. Too much drinking they tell me," had been his explanation when I'd asked why he was at The Shady Rest. "I guess I'm here waiting to die like everybody else."

More often than not he'd reminisce about old friends and the places he'd been. It seemed at times that he was more someplace else than there; but he wanted to share, and I was willing to listen for the few minutes we had.

A few times he'd asked if I could slip him a bottle of gin. I knew I shouldn't, that I'd get fired, but how can you refuse a guy? He gave me the money, and I brought him a pint now and again. He'd always offer to share, and I'd take a friendly swig just for show and maybe another one after that. Then I'd get back to work knowing I'd drink extra at The Dew Drop the next day.

When I'd brought the first bottle, he told me to stop calling him Mr. Jones. I said I'd do that if he'd stop calling me Calvin. I guess by then we'd have both said we were friends, that is if anyone asked, but nobody even knew we shared those few minutes each Sunday.

"Where's home?" Morty asked me one Sunday.

I had to think. "That depends on what you mean. I grew up in Cedar Rapids, but I don't think of it as home. I live here now, so I guess Albuquerque does it."

"No, I mean home—in your heart, where your soul goes when it wants rest."

That one threw me. I told Morty I'd have to think about the answer. He said that was okay, that he'd ask me again.

The next week, soon as I came in the room, he was asking again. "Cal, where's your home."

"I'm still not sure, but I guess The Dew Drop's as close to a home as I got."

"I'd like to go there with you some time."

"Yeah, that would be nice." We both knew it would never happen. That was one of the nights I'd brought him a pint. Maybe I brought it because I knew we were going to have that discussion. Maybe it was just because I liked him.

The Shady Rest wasn't a place I'd want for my home or a place I'd want to end up. I didn't figure Morty liked it much either, but at least for a few minutes each Sunday night, he and I found something worth having there—a moment of friendship, a feeling of sharing, something like home's supposed to be.

"This must be like visiting your old man," Morty observed one Sunday.

"Nah, I like you a hell of a lot better."

There was a silence, something that didn't happen often with Morty.

"You believe in time-travel?" I asked.

He yawned. "I don't know, why?"

"'Cause that's what this feels like—like I'm traveling in time—like for a few minutes each Sunday I'm visiting myself."

Picking up the basket in which I carried my cleaning supplies, I pushed the mop and bucket to the door of the room. I looked back at

Morty and said, "Goodnight." There was no response except the slow rhythm of his breathing.

CHAPTER 17 - RACKING UP THE BALLS

The Dew Drop was quiet. Nobody was talking. Only the click of pool balls as Jonny practiced. Ephraim wasn't singing or strumming. Even Sam was still, his fingers not snapping a rhythm.

Sal was sitting with Ginny. They weren't talking, just holding hands and resting.

Trish left her usual seat and sat down next to me. Hushed, almost whispering, she asked, "Do you guys believe in God?"

It wasn't a question you'd expect—not in a neighborhood bar. Heads turned. Surprised, Jonny missed his shot. "Damn."

Ephraim looked like he wanted to answer, but he took his time, rubbing his chin in thought. I imagined his Amish father with a full beard and a plain black hat making the same gesture. "Growing up," he started, "it wasn't so much believing in God as living with Him. God was just there, part of life, part of day-to-day. Like my grandfather.

"My grandfather was the leader. Everybody looked to him. We didn't have no clergy or no elected head, just all of us believing and praying together. It was like a big family, everybody knowing everybody and doing each for the other. Even if you didn't like …

"We was like family, but in a family there are some voices that get heard more. Grandfather, everybody listened to him. When there was something needed doing; if there were a house to build or a barn to repair, a field that needed mowing, whatever it was, he'd do the suggesting, and everyone else would just agree 'cause he was Grandfather. Nobody ever spoke on it, not out loud. He was just Grandfather—kind of God right there, reminding us of our ways.

"He was my mother's father. His name was Karl, but nobody called him by it, not even his wife or his brothers. Everyone just called him Grandfather. That was their way. Then he had a stroke. A real bad one. Six months or so he hung on, and he died. Even before, before he was dead, when he was still hanging on, it was like God had died. Everybody crying all the time. Even when they was working fields and milking stock, they'd be crying. It was like something was missing, like God wasn't there no more.

"He died. He died in his own bed, in his own home. My grandmother was there. My mother. Her brothers and sister. Everybody. He died. That was the year before my mother…"

There were tears welling in my friend's eyes. He wiped them with his fists, rubbed his hands on his pants, looked at those big hands callused from hard work, at the fingertip on his left hand even more heavily callused by guitar strings. Then he resumed, "Now it's different. I think there's a God; someplace there's got to be. I just wish …" He slapped his right hand on the table. "I just wish I knew where to find Him. I know He ain't in Carlisle's church or even over in the mission; they got good stew and clothes and stuff, but they don't got God.

"I wish …"

There was a long silence. "Damn," Sal broke it. "Yous want a drink?" It was a general question, but it seemed like he was aiming it at Ephraim, who just shook his head and looked down at the table.

"What do you think, Cal?"

I didn't want to answer, didn't want to think about it. Too close to home, to my old man. "I don't know," I mumbled.

"Sure you do," Ginny commented. "A smart guy like you, you got to have some idea."

I could feel the irritation. "I don't like talking about God and religion. That stuff's behind me."

"How's that?" Jonny asked. "How's it behind you?" Jonny came from Ohio and had that flat Midwestern twang. He punctuated his question with the clack of cue ball against another and then the gentle thud of a ball falling into a pocket.

In the silence we could hear that ball running down the gutter and clicking against the others that he had sunk. I looked up, there was only one ball remaining. He dropped another quarter into the slot and started racking. "I guess it's kind of like playing pool." I was making it up as I went. "Sometimes you get to the last ball and you sink it. Other times you rack 'em up again. I just sank that ball and walked away from the table."

"Why?" Trish asked in a serious voice. "Why'd you walk away?"

"It wasn't like Ephraim. We didn't live with God, we lived under Him, at least the way my father interpreted him. He was strict…"

"Your daddy or God?" Ginny asked.

"Both, I guess. Maybe they was the same. I just know there was rules and there was beatin's. Nothin' good, not for me and not for my sister. When I left home it was to get away from both of 'em. God weren't no better than a bully, and my father was the whip in His big hand.

"I don't want any part of either of them, not now and not ever."

"Wha-what about the g-good stuff?" Sam asked. He started snapping his fingers to a syncopated beat. "You kn-know, like mu-music and screwing—"

Sal gave him a look that cut him off.

"And drinking," Tony added. "Don't forget the drinking."

"Most of the time I drink to forget," I said and immediately knew it wasn't true, maybe once, but not anymore.

"Well, I figure there's got to be a God," Jonny put in. "Somebody got to keep racking up the balls."

"What are yous talking about?" Sal asked. "Racking up the balls; that don't make no sense."

"Sure it does," I responded. "We're always gettin' put in a hole. Next thing you know life's going on again. That what you mean, Jonny?"

"Yeah, that's what I mean. Somebody had to rack up them balls."

"God may rack up the balls, but I'm the one sets up the drinks." Sal got up from the table and squeezed behind the bar. "Yous want a drink?"

CHAPTER 18 - NO PLACE ELSE TO GO

I had good reason to appreciate the city's fire department. The reason was Sheila, or more exactly my ability to get Sheila into and out of my room without Mrs. Buthyre's knowledge.

Because hers was a rooming house, our landlady had been required to install a fire escape. Little more than a ladder that climbed the back of the three-story building next to the central rear windows that ventilated the hallways, it allowed Sheila to clamber up the two levels where I would wait, window open and arms extended for her late night arrivals. Again, during the wee hours of the morning, I would open that same window and help her grab hold of the thin metal railings. It was the time in-between ascent and descent that mattered; it was the time we spent in bed.

Sheila was more than a great sex partner; she truly enjoyed it, us. She enjoyed the feel of my scrawny muscles, softly and continuously moving her hands and her lips in exploration. She kissed and caressed and made me feel desirable in ways my puny ego could never have conjured. She sucked on my nipples and licked my ears, she held my penis in her fingers and squeezed with just the right pressure. She spread her legs and moaned with delight at my slightest move. The rhythm of our grand climaxes was mutual and extraordinarily tuned.

She had only two rules, two restrictions: the bleeding-heart-of-Jesus could not watch us and, I could not drink while she was there. So I would cover that mandated picture with a towel and, having prepared myself for each visit with a few quick snorts, I would put what was left of my latest bottle of rye in the dresser and try to ignore the cans of beer in that little fridge. Those were Sheila's only demands. In exchange, my body was loved and celebrated. No gifts were required, no expensive dinners, not even a fancy bedroom. Sheila loved me, she loved my body, and she loved our sex. And, if there is such a thing as truth in alcoholism, she loved her belief, her crazy notion that she was somehow saving me from myself. Sheila was the ultimate co-dependent. And I enjoyed her ministration, her physicality, and, of course, my satisfied sexuality.

On occasion Sheila's arousal-driven vocalizations included words. As her body arched and relaxed in rhythmic syncopation with my own, words of emotion, of love, and of sex would flow in torrents of excitement. "Fuck! Fuck! Yes! OOOOhhhh. I love you. I love this. Fuck! Fuck! Oh, fuck!" At times I would have to interrupt my own exhilaration to ssshh her. Even though our landlady was two floors below and somewhat hard of hearing, there was always that unhappy possibility.

Sheila would laugh and kiss me—sticking her warm, moist tongue into my mouth and welcoming my tongue in hers. Then we would relax for a moment and laugh ever so quietly before plunging once again into the power of our coupling.

Once in a while, not often, but every so often, in the excitement of her vocalizing, Sheila would add a name, Steven. "Oh, Steven, yes, yes!" "Fuck me, Steven. Fuck me and make me hurt." She said those things and probably didn't know she was saying them.

Her words would stop me even in full rut. I would withdraw and ask, "Why are you calling me Steven?"

"I didn't," she'd respond with consternation.

"Yes, you did. Who is he?"

There would be a moment's pause. Then in response but not in answer, she'd go down on me. Sheila was quite a lover, and when she gave head, it was spectacular. Her tongue, lips, and even her palate were called into action. And me, being a drinker and sometimes a little soft, really appreciated her going down. It aroused me like nothing else she did could. Those times, when I would cum, it would be like something beyond limits. Sheila would at those moments swallow full and clean and then, when I was exhausted and flaccid, she would carefully wipe her lips with her fingers and suck them like my chizz was some kind of holy nectar.

Those times, those glorious moments, only occurred after she had christened me Steven.

Naturally, I thought of telling her that she had uttered the name even when she had not. It was a great temptation, but something held back. I feared she would recognize the deception, that it would damage or even end the glory of her desire to satisfy me.

***

Clean With Grace was hiring part-time help, and Ephraim and I were as part-time as anyone could want. Even better, they were hiring late night cleaners and inventory takers. Realistically, we knew that neither of us would be at our best late at night, not after an evening at The Dew Drop, but we also knew that most of the applicants would be other drinkers or undocumented Mexicans trying to hold down as many jobs as they could. So we went down one morning and applied.

"This job is at Beck and Beck," the woman said with a sneer of authority. "Are you familiar with their establishment?"

"Sure," I half lied, "I know it well." Actually, I'd never set foot in the place; what would I need in an office supply store? But I did know where Beck and Beck's shiny new store had taken over half a block. I knew where the construction had been dragging on for close to a year. Evidently it was going to open soon, and that meant a thorough cleaning and inventory. "It would be a great place to work," I added just to gild the lily. I smiled my best smile, and Sheila smiled back. Of course I didn't know her name then. I did know she was gorgeous, more gorgeous and sexier than I had ever imagined. Deep brown eyes that matched the brown light perfection of her hair. Lips, carefully glossed with just enough size to be welcoming and not so much as to be a pout. A tailored suit saying success without brag.

I didn't know her name, but there was a spark in those smiles that I would come to know so well.

Sheila was the mainstay of Beck and Beck; she had been since the original Mr. Beck had died leaving his business to his two children, George Beck, Jr. and Miss Betsy Beck.

Beck and Beck hated each other and only Sheila could navigate the roiling waters between them. Despite those difficulties and the increased competition from office supply chains, Sheila had grown Beck and Beck until this new, larger store was justified. Understandably, she was proud of her accomplishment and wanted to make sure every member of that cleaning and inventory effort would do the job correctly. That she was drawing on the least of the work force didn't faze her. "Have you done inventory work before?" she asked in the most non-threatening voice.

"Yes," I half lied again. Hadn't I done my share of inventory control at Heinrich's Real Deli? "Of course not with office supplies," I added to make myself sound more believable. "And I've got lots of experience cleaning," that said to bring a bit more honesty to the situation.

"I see ..." She looked me up and down. "Are you a drinker?" she asked, this time in a no-nonsense tone.

How to answer? I could lie, but I knew she'd not believe me. I could tell the truth, but I knew that it might cost me the job and I sorely needed the money. What if I say yes and she asks me how much? "Well, ma'am, I have to admit I do like my beer." Better to leave the whiskey and wine out of the discussion.

"You do? Does that mean there will—"

"Be a problem?" I interrupted her. "No, ma'am; I'll get the job done. I drink for pleasure, but I don't drink to escape or nothing like that." I could imagine my parents guffawing at that one but they were in Iowa, and the job was here in Albuquerque. I tried one of my most ingratiating smiles and hoped that she would smile back.

"Just remember," she said sternly enough for me to know it would not be true, "you show up drunk, and you're out of there for good."

"Yes, ma'am," I went along with the farce. "I do need the work." It was intended to reassure.

"Judging from your clothes, I would guess you do." And I was wearing my best, torn and frayed as they were. It made me blush. Anyway, I knew I was hired. At the time that was all I had wanted.

***

The chemistry was immediate. I became Sheila's project; her goal, my redemption and sobriety. I played it perfectly, not by intent but by my own internal rollercoaster, one night hard working and sober and the next wavering and weaving, but always, always smiling and happy to see her, happy to reassure that I was doing, was going to give, my best.

"I'm sorry" worked so well with her. "Sheila, I really am sorry." It worked again and again.

Soon sex became part of the equation. The more unpredictable but apparently repentant I became the more physical Sheila became. Kissing and fondling at first and then rollicking sex on her desk, a mahogany giant, a token on which she had insisted and to which Beck and Beck immediately agreed.

"When I saw this desk, I knew I wanted this moment," she said as she slipped out of her clothes. It was the first time I had actually been in that office.

"Uh huh," I muttered as I pulled off my underwear. It was a brand new pair, boxers, light blue. My new dark blue shirt and jeans were already on the floor. Only my socks were still on. They, too, were blue. Blue was Sheila's favorite color.

The night before, as we were all leaving, Sheila had given me three crisp new twenties. "Tomorrow, come to work dressed nice," she said; "I have something special planned."

She had winked, and I smiled in response. "I bet you do," I responded.

"Something really special."

"Hmmm."

In the background I could hear some of the other workers, who were waiting for Sheila to let us out, muttering. They had figured out what was going on. Sheila was oblivious, but I could feel their combined disapproval, amusement, and envy.

Mounting her on that massive desk I, too, had become oblivious. I knew that Ephraim was cleaning the new bathrooms getting them ready for the official opening only two days away. I knew that Ginny was counting legal pads and affixing those stickers with price and barcode. And I knew some of the other men and women who were hard at work. But I didn't care; the only thing that mattered was the feeling of power and the urgency of my need. My prick was hard and demanding relief.

"This is better than booze, isn't it?" Sheila asked just as I was about to penetrate.

"Yeah, sure," I answered not wanting to think about anything but the immediate moment.

"Mmmmm." I could hear her satisfaction even before I had found her vagina, even before my fingers had searched out her clitoris or my mouth had found her tit. That should have been a signal, a warning that this desirable woman really did have an agenda where drinking was concerned. But who cared? She was desirable—well built with smooth skin that seemed to glisten in merry anticipation, a smile that warmed my heart, and a voice that promised more.

Surprising myself with the force of it, I thrust myself into her. Immediately our bodies took up the rhythm of sex. Our hands and mouths danced in appreciation of each other's bodies. We fucked and fucked again. We loved and we touched and we kissed — everywhere. It was great. The only way it could have been better was to have a drink or maybe a nice glass of wine. I made the suggestion, and Sheila pushed me off. "I don't drink," she said in a tone that allowed no contradiction, "and you don't drink around me. Is that understood?"

"Yes, ma'am," I answered and then burst into laughter.

"What are you laughing at?"

"Calling you ma'am. I mean we're lying here naked, and I'm calling you ma'am."

"You aren't."

"I just did," I said.

"No, you're not naked; you still have your socks on."

We were both laughing.

Later, when Sheila was letting the crew out of the building, none of them would look at me. Even as we walked back to Mrs. Buthyre's, Ephraim wasn't talking. It was only when we had climbed the stairs and were going to our separate rooms that he spoke. "I know," he said.

"I know you do."

"It isn't a problem or anything…"

"But?"

"We were all working."

"Yeah." I knew where he was going, but I was going to play dumb. "So?"

"It feels like you're taking advantage—"

"Of Sheila?"

"No, not of her, of us."

"Oh."

"It seems—"

"Yeah, sure." I went into my room and closed the door.

The next night, Sheila and I humped on the desk again. I knew Ephraim was ticked as we again walked home, but I figured it was all right since the next day Beck and Beck would be open, and our temp jobs would be over. I assumed that Sheila would be over, too.

I was wrong. Two days later I got a message that Sheila wanted to see me at the store. I wanted more of what she had to give, so I went to see her.

"I've been thinking about you."

"Me, too."

She handed me a little box tied with a blue ribbon. Confused, I held it. "Aren't you going to open it?"

"Sure." I tore off the ribbon. Inside was a silver lighter. It was engraved with her name.

"So you'll think about me."

"Every time I light up."

"Every time you light up."

She gave me a job on the Beck and Beck cleaning staff, nothing too difficult or too high paying, but enough.

"We can't have sex here," she informed me as she patted that grand desk.

"Oh." I could hear my own disappointment.

"Where do you live?" I told her and I told her about Mrs. Buthyre and about those bleeding-heart pictures.

"Can I get in without running into your landlady?"

We talked about the fire escape and times and about Ephraim and how he might have an objection or two.

If he did, he got over it because he never said anything about Sheila's visits, and I never asked.

***

The sex was good—better than good, but there was something missing. We shared nothing except our bodies. Once or twice a week Sheila climbed the fire escape and we screwed—wonderful, exciting sex. But we didn't talk much, we didn't go out, and we didn't have contact with other people. In fact, we hardly ever mentioned anyone else; that is except Steven, whoever he was. More and more often that name would escape her lips during the intensity of our fucking. Then, when I would mention it, when I would point out that slip, Sheila would give me head, insane, excited head. Those were the best times of all. Still.

I suggested that she come down to The Dew Drop, that she meet the rest of the family, those who had not worked at Beck and Beck. Sheila refused over and over again. Finally, if only to quiet me, she showed up.

It was a Thursday evening. She came in dressed like the businesswoman she was, nodded to the people she knew, acted as if she barely knew me, ordered a coke, sipped it for a while and talked with Sal about how difficult it was to own a small business. Nobody else spoke; Jonny stopped playing pool and sat quietly sipping a beer and watching Sheila. Sharon stiffened in silent envy and drank her vodka and tonic too quickly. She was outclassed and resented it.

I gulped the last of my rye and ginger, sputtering and almost choking on my fear of her reaction, but Sheila said nothing. I wanted to order a coke or maybe a coffee, but I ended up saying, "A beer, Sal, a nice cold glass."

He looked at me with a smirk and drew a glass with just the right head. "This one's on the house." I knew his jokes about my coughing and choking would cost me more than the sixty cents.

Sheila was the center of attention and clearly in the wrong place. Finishing her coke, she smiled benignly—one could have imagined a queen making her progress. "Thank you," she said to Sal and offered her hand, which he took uncomfortably. "If you're ever in need of office supplies, a computer, anything, you stop by Beck and Beck and ask for me." She smiled but pointedly didn't mention her name.

"Thank you," Sal seemed to stumble over the simple words. He looked at Ginny and nodded at her in discomfort.

Two nights later, when Sheila came clambering up to my room, I was still uncomfortable. She smiled at me, not sweetly, but like she was pissed. "That went well," she said.

Not knowing what else to do, I started disrobing. She did the same, and soon I was licking the perspiration from beneath her arms, my teeth tearing gently at the stubble, my taste buds savoring the saltiness of her being.

The embarrassment of The Dew Drop lay forgotten in the pile of our clothes and the sweat exertion of our sex. She never returned to the bar, and I never again asked.

***

Sex is a strange goddess. No matter how well satisfied she seems to always demand more. If Sheila and I were not to have a social component to our relationship, if we could not be comfortable hanging out at The Dew Drop, then I conjured another desire. I expressed it in the most concerned fashion: the danger of that fire escape, especially in rain or worse; the unfairness of her having to climb like a common thief, the inequality of my having the comfort of my home, my room. Clearly, I could not and she should not afford a hotel. That would make no sense. But perhaps I could come to her, at least on the bad nights when it was dangerous.

I begged and pleaded. "You make me feel like I'm a bum." "Don't you trust me? Are you afraid I'll steal something?" "I thought you cared … about me."

Finally Sheila acquiesced. "It's just an apartment, nothing much," she said dismissively.

"I know, but it's your apartment. If nothing else it will help me to know you better."

"Oh, you're planning to snoop."

"Of course not," I demurred my feelings a bit hurt. "I just …"

She laughed and kissed me on the forehead like a mother teasing her son. "You're so easy."

It was my turn to laugh—not happily nor with embarrassment but in some discomfort. Still, I was satisfied; she had agreed. We planned for the following Tuesday.

That morning, having no extra cash, I took a few dollars from my envelope, from the money I was slowly saving for a trip back to Cedar Rapids. Better spent on Sheila than my parents. I thought of how disapproving my parents would have been if they had known about us. Perhaps they wouldn't mind my sleeping with someone, but my boss—I could hear Dad's voice in my head. I chuckled to myself at the thought of his garrumphing tone and condemning comments.

The money was to buy something, something special, to bring with me. I wanted it to be a bottle of wine, but I knew that would upset and anger. No, it would have to be something else, something she could accept. Chocolate. I went to the Godiva store and bought a pound—more than we could eat and far more than I could afford.

I asked for blue ribbon, which they didn't have; but it was a handsome box, something a proper boyfriend might bring. I held it toward Sheila as she opened the door.

She took the box absently and put it on a small table by the door. "You shouldn't have." I could tell she meant it.

"I just—"

"No matter." Was she talking about my explanation, the candy, or me? I didn't know. What I did know was that her "nothing much" apartment was far more than I had imagined. Very modern and stylish, like something from a magazine. I knew I didn't belong.

"This is something." I drew the words out to let her know I was impressed.

"It does for me, not that I spend that much time…"

"A lot nicer than my—"

She laughed, not letting me finish.

There was a piano, a baby grand, black and shiny with pictures in silver frames. I walked over and looked at those photographs. There was one of the Becks when old Mr. Beck was still alive. He had written on it, "Sheila, To my office daughter who brings me joy, Horace Beck."

"That's very nice," I commented pointing to the photograph.

"He liked me. I think he had a crush on me, too—one of those senile things. He left me … That's how I bought this. I was fond of him, too." It wasn't embarrassment that interrupted her sentences but a breezy indifference. "Let's go upstairs."

"Upstairs?"

"To the bedroom, silly."

"Oh." I started to move toward her and then pulled back. There was a photograph of another family, two adults and two children. The woman looked just like Sheila. "Who's this?" I asked.

"My family. That's me when I was ten or eleven."

"You were a cute kid." I stared at the picture. "Where are they now?"

"My parents? They're dead. Mom died of cancer; Dad a heart attack the next year. I was at college. I barely got home for the funeral."

"Is this your brother?"

"Yes." Her tone was so flat I couldn't imagine why. I waited for her to say more, but she didn't.

"Does he live around here?"

"No." The same affectless tone.

"It doesn't—"

"I don't want to talk about him."

"Oh, sorry, I didn't …" I was still staring at the photograph.

"I'd get rid of that photo, but it's the best one I have of my parents."

"Oh."

"He killed them."

"I thought—"

"The doctors didn't know, didn't understand. When he was arrested, that was the cancer, that was the heart attack. He killed them as if he'd used a gun or—"

"Arrested?" She stood mute so I asked again, "Arrested?"

"There was this little girl." She sobbed ever so lightly. Sniffed. Resumed. "He molested her, raped her. Said he couldn't help …" She balled her hands into fists and rubbed them into her eyes. "Damn him!" she shouted. She sat on the nearest chair and cried. I wanted to go to her, to comfort, but I stood a statue next to that piano and watched her battle with her own demons.

"I'm responsible," she sobbed. "I should have stopped him, told, done something."

I waited; it seemed like forever.

"I was his first," Sheila finally moaned. "His baby sister. He said he loved…"

This time I forced myself to move to her. I knelt next to the chair and tried to take her hand. She pulled it away.

"If I had told … If I had been better … Steven, Steven," she said his name in such a whimpering voice. "I hate him. I miss him. I love …"

Slowly I got up and went to the door. "I'm sorry," I said softly, knowing that she didn't hear. I went out into the night. Wearily, I made my way to The Dew Drop. It was way across town; that didn't matter; I had no place else to go.

That night I put the silver lighter, the one with her name, into my Cedar Rapids envelope. Maybe I'd keep it. Maybe I'd pawn it. One thing—I wasn't going to carry it around to remind me.

CHAPTER 19 - DANCE

We didn't dance—not in Cedar Rapids. Jan and I might have wanted to, but our father would have none of it. "It's against God's law," he thundered, and for us the earth quaked and shook.

"Harry," Mom would say in her quieting voice, but it did no good. He'd send us to our rooms to pray for forgiveness. Ours was a perpetual state of sin.

The phys ed teacher, Mr. Mackey, had decided to teach eighth and ninth grades to square dance. It was for parents' night. No matter. God's law was, and that was sufficient. While our classmates honored their partners and promenaded the hall, my sister and I ran laps in the November cold.

Rob Parsite was in Jan's grade. I asked how come he wasn't running with us. After all, his father was the minister; surely God's law applied at least as much to him as to us. Rob laughed. "I didn't tell the old man," he explained. "Why would you go and do something dumb like that?"

I have no idea if my sister Jan ever danced wherever she has ended up in her life. I still didn't dance in Albuquerque. I did, however, like to go to the street fairs and hang out around the dancing. A bottle hidden in a paper bag, wandering around swaying as if to the music was what Ephraim and I called an evening out, doing something different.

We all gravitated to those nights in Old Town. Even if Sal did keep The Dew Drop open, we were going out and having some fun. Randomly, we'd circulate, run into one another and nod as if we were taking part in an important social event; then we'd take another sip from our paper-sacked bottles. We might have stopped to chat, not to say anything we hadn't already said a hundred times at The Dew Drop, just to say something, but we were afraid. The cops might notice, better to move along.

Just being there was fun. Being part of the action. People, all dressed up and feeling important milled around and bought cups of strong coffee, beers, and tacos. Teenagers would stop us and ask if we'd buy them wine coolers and would offer us cigarettes in exchange. Younger kids ran and played tag. They yelled and teased and jumped around.

Occasionally they'd bump into us.

"Watch yourself!"

"Dumb drunk."

Whatcha doing, Mr. Bum?" They weren't pleasant kids, full of their own excitement. I wanted to trip one, but again, there were those cops.

We didn't panhandle. We weren't bums, not those of us who hung out at The Dew Drop. We worked jobs and lived in regular places. People knew us. We knew us. We weren't the bottom of the barrel, but still we had to watch out for the police.

Every now and then we'd see somebody we knew, not from The Dew Drop but from real life, somebody we'd worked with or for, perhaps a regular customer at the deli or at the Chinese. We'd nod, and they'd nod, but never words.

Monica, whose real name was something else, was usually there. She and a photographer would go up to people who looked important or maybe like tourists. It didn't seem like much of a job, her pestering people who would rather be dancing; but the next day there would something in the paper.

One time Ephraim and I went up to her and asked, "How come you don't interview us?"

She laughed and turned away.

"Hey, Monica," I yelled to draw attention, "how come you don't come by The Dew Drop anymore?"

She turned back, smiled almost sweetly, and gave me the finger. Just then I saw a blue uniform moving in our direction. I grabbed Ephraim and pulled him away. We wove our way into the crowd. When I turned to look, the cop was putting somebody in handcuffs. Who knows?

Once Sal and Ginny started their thing, they'd show up at those dances, too. The first time it really surprised most of us. It meant Sal was paying a substitute to work the bar even when he knew nobody would be around. Obviously, the relationship was getting serious.

There would be breaks in the regular dancing during which a mariachi band would play. Eager Mexican couples would then come to the center of the Plaza—the señoritas dressed in those bright, bouncing, swirling dresses with flowers in their hair and the men in their short jackets, tight black pants, and heeled boots. While the music—guitars, violins, and trumpets—filled the plaza and echoed off the adobe buildings, the gaily clad couples danced with dramatic stomping and gestures.

A lot of the crowd would use those breaks to drift towards the food and drink vendors. But I always pushed toward that wonderfully whirling and surging music. I could feel my feet wanting to take part. As if guided by a mind of their own, they'd tap and stomp. Every now and then a teenager nursing a beer and a sense of importance noticed my tapping and pointed me out to his buddies. "Look at the drunk," he'd say and they'd laugh like it was some great joke.

"Leave him alone, he just likes the music," Ephraim would speak up for me.

"Another drunk," one of the teens would shout. "Maybe they're lovers." Another round of laughter, even harder.

I didn't mind. For the moment I was back in Cedar Rapids, and I wasn't the kid running laps and looking a fool. I was part of things; I was part of the music, part of the party. And the old man couldn't stop me.

Back at The Dew Drop having a nightcap before we headed home, we'd talk about the celebrations. One night Trish said, "You know you dance pretty good."

I blushed like a kid. I didn't believe she meant it, but I blushed anyway.

"Yeah, you really do," Tony added.

"Wish I'd been there to see it," Jonny put in. "I had a big game at O'Grady's."

"You missed a great party," Chip said, "a really great party."

We nodded in agreement.

"Maybe next time," Jonny said. We all knew he wouldn't make it. Jonny played pool. For him that was enough. In a way I envied him—at least he had something that was enough.

CHAPTER 20 - THE TROPHY GOES TO

Uncle Hiram wasn't pleased, and he had let Hunter know. Six bars had signed up for the Black Orchid Softball League. Uniforms had been purchased by bar owners and equipment by the company. Free beer had been promised to motivate regulars to form teams and even in some cases to practice; all in hopes of media coverage, in hopes of increased business. And nobody was interested, not the press, not the local television, not even radio.

"'Who wants to watch a bunch of drunks trying to act like athletes?'" That was Sky quoting his boss. "The old man was furious. The whole thing is off.

"Hunter's been promoted," he continued. "Now vice president in charge of inventory. He tried to argue with the boss, but uncle said, 'Vice president in charge of inventory or vice president in charge of empties, your choice.' I laughed so hard I almost peed myself." Then he did laugh, that big barrel-chested laugh.

"Old Hiram, he says I'm supposed to do the deliveries now—all myself. Guess that my promotion, do more work.

"I tell him I need help. He's not happy, but my cousin Clay work with me now. Clay's a good worker. He's from Pueblo in Taos and know how to work."

That was true; Clay worked his butt off, which didn't make us any happier. Gone was the opportunity to get free beers from Sky. He didn't need our help.

"How how about some b-brew for us?" Sam asked. He was broke, had been dry since the night before and was feeling the need.

Sky elaborately scratched his balls. "Can't do, no more. Clay needs to get paid. Have to take care of my cousin."

"You guys don't look like cousins." Even without tequila, Chip was working his way to anger.

"What you mean don't look like cousins. We're both Injans. We all look the same."

Maybe it was meant as a joke, but only Riley laughed. "You got him good, Chief."

"I'm not chief, just truck driver." Easygoing Sky had disappeared. This guy was now an administrator, a boss. It was clear; he'd laugh at us, but not with us. "I got lots of beer to deliver. You finished, Clay?"

"Yes, sir."

Chip turned his anger on Sal. "What the hell's gonna happen with the team?"

"I don' know." Sal busied himself behind the bar.

"Come on, ya gotta know something."

"What about the cheerleaders?" Sharon added her two cents.

"Yeah, we've been practicing so hard." We knew that Ginny's complaint would at least get a response.

"I'll talk to the other bar owners and then we'll see what Black Orchid will do for us. Yous knows I got my money in those uniforms and the beers I gave you at practice. I'm not happy any more than yous guys."

"So why didn't you say nothin'?"

"To who? To Sky? That Indian's got nothin' to do with it. He does deliveries not decidin'."

Sal looked over at me. "Yous want a drink?"

"Yeah, sure." I put some money on the bar. He put down my usual, made change, half smiled, and said, "Enjoys yourself." I dropped the change in Ephraim's bowl and took a sip. Things were back to normal— almost.

The grumbling didn't stop. We drank. Ephraim sang. He sang about disappointment:

"You should've said no,

You should've gone home,

You should have thought twice before you let it all go."

His singing didn't help the mood any.

We drank some more. Carol came in. We told her the news and she started to cry. That got us even farther into the dumps. So we all ordered another round to comfort her. Greg even stood one for Chip, which calmed him down some.

The only one who wasn't drinking was Tom. "I'm too pissed to drink."

"We're all bummed out," I responded.

"No, you don't get it. I'd given up drinking. I was sober. I liked A.A.

Then you guys and this damned softball thing. Now I'm back on the sauce and … Jesus I'm pissed. For nothing. For fuckin' nothing." He slammed his fist onto the table. Greg's glass jumped, fell to the floor in a splash of beer and glass.

"Shit, that was a full glass."

"God damn it," Sal yelled. " Yourse sober, yous clean it up." He threw a rag at Tom, who caught it, got on his knees and started cleaning up the mess.

From the floor Tom called, "Sal, give Greg another glass. I'll pay for it."

"How a-about one one for me, t-too?" Sam asked.

"Go to hell." Tom's anger was clear.

Somehow the whole scene seemed outrageously funny to Tony and Chuck. They started laughing. Pretty soon the rest of us joined in. Ephraim put a top on it with another rendition of "Take Me Out to the Ballgame."

"Hey, Sal, you got any Crackerjacks?" Chip asked.

"Nah. I got some more pretzels."

"Hey, let's go buy some Crackerjacks." Trish was now in a good mood.

"Yeah," Carol added, "and we can get Sal a box of Oneida Biscuits."

"Yous guys don't make no sense."

"God damn all of ya," Tom blurted. He stormed out of the bar.

***

They had a meeting. We weren't there, and Sal wasn't talking about it. Maybe he told Ginny, but if he did, she didn't share. Instead we heard about it indirect. Smyth, who owned The Watering Hole, was one of the people at the meeting. Five of the six bar owners and Uncle Hiram Hoffmyer, the boss of Black Orchid, were there. Smyth talked about it at home. His son Ralph, who was one of Chuck's regular weed customers at the bodega, told Chuck – probably expecting some extra dope.

Chuck waited till Sal was out of The Dew Drop; he and Ginny had gone out to dinner, which was their newest thing. Sal's latest substitute bartender was this scrawny punk, Troy. Troy was always bragging about the women he had, which nobody believed. Tom had made some comment about the women of Troy. Most of us didn't get it, but after that we called the guy TWOT, which we rhymed with hoot just so as not to offend.

"Have I got the story," Chuck began; "I know what happened at that meeting.

"The old man, you know Hoffmyer over at Black Orchid, he offered each bar two free kegs if they'd just forget it all. Which was fine with most of them, but Cochran wanted more.

"And Sal objected, too. He said Hunter had promised all the guys free beer at the games so they'd have to use the free beer for their regulars or there'd be a lot of pissin'. One of the other guys said that would just be too damn bad, but Sal and Cochran held out till the old guy said, 'I'll give you each four kegs. You decide who gets what. Give them some or all or none. How's that?'

"Well, they all agreed to four kegs, but Johnson. He's the one owns The Mountain View over on the East Side, says they got to agree how they're gonna do it otherwise the regulars would talk to one another and somebody'd have a problem or somebody'd like look too good. Anyway, they agreed they'd each have a big day when they'd give out two kegs to the regulars, which seemed pretty good.

"Then Lovelace says they got to go with the same day so's no one can go from bar to bar dependin' on when they was givin' out the beer."

"That makes sense," Shelly said. I wished he hadn't said anything. Truth was, you could somehow forget how bad he smelled, and then he'd open his mouth and remind you he was around.

"Last Saturday of the month," Tony interrupted. That was something we all already knew, free beer the last Saturday. The news had spread like wildfire.

"Yeah," Chuck continued. "Then Sal does something nobody expects. 'We got these uniforms and teams and even cheerleaders,' he says; 'so maybe we should let them play a few games.'"

"That must have been Ginny's doin'," Carol comment.

We all laughed at that idea, which made TWOT ask what were talking about that was so funny. Chip says, "It ain't none of your business." And everybody says yeah and that's right so he goes back to washing glasses.

"So what did they say?" Tom wants to know.

"They says we should have some games that Saturday, earlier in the day, make a big thing of it."

"So we're gonna play?" Carol demanded.

"Looks like. Course not the whole nine yards, but we'll play."

"What about that trophy?" I was surprised that Ephraim cared.

"I didn't hear nothin' about no trophy, but we're gonna play and we're havin' the beer, and that's pretty good."

We all agreed, which again got Troy's attention. "You guys up to something?" he asked.

"Yeah, we're up to drinking free," Tony said, and we all laughed, which made TWOT look really uneasy.

"Look, guys, I just do what Sal tells me." He turned red-faced.

We had another good laugh.

***

Later that evening, when Sal and Ginny got back, Carol asked him if the rumors were true.

"Where did yous guys hear that?" Sal was busy counting the till and making sure Troy hadn't shortchanged him.

"Never mind that; is it true?"

"Yeah, it's true. Our team's playin' the joiks from The Oasis, so yous better be ready for 'em. Yous lose to Cochran, and yous can forget no beer."

We laughed. Chip, who as usual was smoking away, got into one of those coughing fits where he couldn't get his breath. He was bent over hacking himself blue.

"And yous," Sal continued, "cut them coffin nails; yous coughin' enough already. How the devil yous gonna play thoid base bent over like that?"

More laughter, and coughing.

"You gonna come to the game?" Tom asked in an uncharacteristically good mood. He was feeling no pain, which gave Tony, Chip, and me something more to celebrate. At least we didn't have to feel so guilty about talking Tom off that wagon.

"Yeah, I'll be there. In fact, The Dew Drop is takin' the day off. Just the game and the party after so yous damn well better play good."

"How about some of that beer now?" Tom asked.

"Yous want a drink?"

"Yeah, sure."

"Then yous pay for it. I ain't givin' the stuff away."

There was a groan. Not that anyone was surprised, just that we were hoping.

"Hey, Sal." Ephraim spoke up.

"Yeah."

"What about that trophy?"

"What trophy?"

"You know, the one for the softball team. How's the old man going to decide which team gets the trophy?"

"We didn't talk about it."

Don't you want it?"

Damn, Ephraim wants that thing bad. I wonder why.

"Why do you care so much? I asked.

"'Cause I never had a trophy in my life. I kind of thought ..." His voice trailed off and he absently strummed his guitar.

"Not even for your singing?" Greg asked half seriously.

"Nah."

Greg turned to the barkeep. "Then what about that trophy? We got to win it for our buddy, right guys?"

Only Tom responded with a half-hearted "right."

"Right guys!?" Greg demanded more loudly.

That time we all yelled in agreement and started clapping like a bunch of kids.

"Trophy, trophy, trophy." Ginny shimmied around the room trying to lead us in that one-word cheer.

"What the hell, why not?" Sal said as he grabbed for her and missed. "I'll call Hiram up tomorrow morning and ask him what's going on."

"Yeah!" The feeling was genuine. It was immediately followed by the need for a drink. Celebration was called for.

***

The big Saturday came. We gathered at The Dew Drop. Breakfast, no real booze, just one lousy beer each. Breakfast burritos. Good choice, but the butterflies. "How about another one, just to settle our stomachs?"

"God damn drunks," Sal muttered. "After I buys yous breakfast and everything."

"We are not a bunch of drunks; we're your customers."

"What kind of a bar is this?"

"Come on, Sal."

"Hey, TWOT, what about you? No tip next time."

"Whatya mean you jerks don't tip me nothin' anyway?"

"I'll bet Cochran's lettin' his guys hit that keg."

"Yous want something to drink, have coffee." Sal grabbed the pot and started around the room. At least it was fresh, but the last time that pot had been washed … it still had that heavy smell.

Meanwhile, Ephraim was ignoring us. He was staring at the window, maybe counting cobwebs or studying the pattern of the smudges that hadn't been washed off for who knew how long. Suddenly he turned to Sal. "Did Hoffmyer say anything about that trophy?"

Sal looked at him with this look that said, "Why are you bothering me?" But out loud he said, "Why do yous care so much?"

"I just do. Is he putting it up or not?"

"Yeah, he is. The best team gets it."

"How come?" *Leave it to Chip to ask a dumb question.*

"'Cause he paid for it already so he figured he might as well."

"We're going to win it. We have to." Ephraim was suddenly an emphatic little kid full of hope and expectation.

"That's right," Tom said. "We are gonna win."

"Go team! Go team. Win, win, win!" Ginny, Bev, and Sharon cheered together.

"You can do it, team," added Trish, full of enthusiasm even if she didn't know the cheers.

"What do you say, Sal?" Greg put in.

"I say, yous guys win it and I'll put it up there." He pointed to a shelf.

"I meant are you gonna spring for free drinks?"

"Don't go pressin' your luck. Yous gettin' the beer yous gettin'."

"It don't matter, we're gonna win." Carol was standing feet spread apart and looking more intense and more sober than any of us had ever seen her.

"Shit, Carol," I said, "you know you look just like your brother like you're ready to get some bad ass and throw him down."

Carol laughed. It was infectious, so was her attitude. Suddenly we were all of one mind, and we were going to win. We were ready except for one thing.

"Hey, Sal, how about one more beer?"

***

Late that afternoon, we were sitting around, feeling no pain and wishing there were more free brew. We'd emptied those two kegs and a lot more to say nothing of the hard stuff that wasn't part of the deal. But we'd won and won big so we were pretty damn happy, except for Chip, who figured he deserved at least one shot of tequila, especially since he'd made that great catch to end the fourth inning.

"You ain't gettin' no damn tequila in my bar," Sal had told him, "catch or no catch." But he did slip him an extra shot of rye. Sal was really happy even if he was trying to make light of everything.

So we were getting ready to say, "Shit, we're out of beer and money." when Hunter showed up. He had this medium-sized box that he handed over to Sal and said, "My uncle told me to get this over to you. He turned to the roomful of us, "You guys did great, and Black Orchid is real proud to have sponsored your softball team."

Sal was trying to say something about having done most of the sponsoring himself, but he didn't get a chance before Hunter was out the door. "Damn that joik. I should never ..."

"Let me open that for you," Ginny sidled up to Sal and flashed him a smile. It took her a minute to get the box open and pull out a trophy. Once it was out of the wrapping, she kissed it and then handed it to Sal. He told Greg to get him a chair to stand on so he could put that trophy on the shelf, but Carol stopped him. "Don't we all get to look at it?"

"Yeah, sure." He handed her this silver colored thing. It's pretty decent looking with a guy swinging a bat on top.

Carol held it out so she could read the words: "BLACK ORCHID SOFTBALL WINNERS, PROUDLY PRESENTED BY BLACH ORCHID DISTRIBUTING TO:"

"They didn't even put The Dew Drop on it." Chip fumed.

"That's nothin'; they even misspelled Black," Carol pointed out.

"How cheap can it get?" Tom spoke the general consensus.

Ephraim grabbed the trophy out of Carol's hand and held it up. "I don't care what any of you say," he told us, "at least we won." He had this shit-eating grin that made me feel as warm as all the free beer I'd swilled.

Sal put the trophy up on that shelf, and Ginny said, "Let's have one more cheer." She and Bev started something about "Dew Drop, Dew Drop, Don't drop the ball." They were jumping up and down and acting like kids. Trish was trying to keep up with them, so she sounded like an echo.

***

On the way home, Ephraim said, "You know it really feels good."

"What does?"

"Winning. I never won nothing before."

"Yeah, I don't suppose I did either."

It wasn't till the next day when Sal called Cochran to rub it in that we learned the truth. Hoffmyer had sent Hunter out with six of those cheap trophies. He'd even sent one to The Good Night Inn, and their team hadn't even shown up to play Mountain View.

Somehow it didn't matter. We were winners, and that was good to know.

CHAPTER 21 - THREE SANTAS

It had been a misery of a day—dark and blowing sleet, which explains why so many of us had already taken our daily refuge in The Dew Drop Inne. By evening's fall it seemed that everyone wanted a drink, especially the guys who had been standing outside all afternoon ringing bells, and wishing Merry Christmas to shoppers who dropped change into kettles and cans. In they half trooped and half staggered, three hapless Santas, employed for the season by charities that existed in large part to help the scraggly of the world.

Shelly came in first. It was his day off from the Maxi Triple X. What better way to spend it than making extra money. "Ho, ho, ho," he called as he entered the bar. His breath, as always smelling of stale cheese, filled the room.

Ephraim made a sour face, strummed an extra chord, and went back to singing *Jingle Bells*.

I chugged some beer and said, "Ho, ho, ho to you." Somehow that struck Shelly as humorous.

Slamming his fist on the bar, he demanded, "Sal, a drink for Santa or on the bad boys' list you go."

"No free drinks for Santa or no one else."

"Sal, Sal, where's your holiday spirit?"

"Yous want spirits, yous pay for 'em."

Grappling under his heavy red jacket trimmed in white, Shelly fished out his wallet and slapped money on the bar.

Chuck was next to enter. He seemed to be shivering with the cold and wet. He shook himself dry. *A Santa dog*. I couldn't help smirking at the thought.

The third Santa was new. He came in with Chuck. "So who's the elf?" Chip asked.

"That ain't no elf; that's Mr. Claus himself." Tony was going to be difficult.

"They can't all be no Santa," Chip responded.

"At least they're all in uniform," Captain observed in one of his sudden bursts of interest. Most of the time he seemed locked in a different world—one bounded by VA approved medications.

He suddenly got up from the table. "I'd better inspect the troops."

Captain hadn't been around for a while. His appearances in our world were sporadic. "They had me caged," he had explained to those of us who had been around earlier in the day. "Something about the sporting goods store."

Every now and again the VA would let Captain out. His medications in order, he played the role of military officer inspecting troops and issuing orders that no one followed, but he did no harm. Unfortunately, Captain never stayed on those pills. Once they had worn off he would get into trouble. Often he'd go looking for weapons. "I got to patrol the perimeter," he'd explain. There wasn't a gun shop, shooting range, or sporting goods store that he hadn't disrupted. Each time landing him back on the locked wards.

"Captain, you got to stay away from guns," Tom had one time said to him as if it would make a difference.

"I know. I know. I didn't mean no harm."

He never did. But he couldn't stay away from those guns.

"Name's Tim. Merry Christmas." The new guy held out his white-gloved hand toward Sal.

"Yous want a drink?"

"Yeah, sure, with a beer."

"That's what we soive here, Mr. Santa." Sal served him.

"What about me?" Chuck asked.

"Yous got money?"

"All these guys should go on report," Captain roared. "There ain't a clean uniform in the bunch."

"That's 'cause we've been workin' all day," Chuck explained. "It wasn't easy neither."

Captain ignored him, shook his head in disdain, and went to the john.

"Tell me about it," Shelly added. "I was over at the Hilton. They wouldn't even let me get under that awning."

"How'd ya do?" Tony asked.

"Actually, pretty good. I guess people felt sorry for me, Santa standin' in the rain that way. Now if I don't get sick or nothin'." He took off his gloves and rubbed his hands as if he could warm them.

Chuck pulled out a small wad of bills and put them on the bar. "Hey, Santa, you buying for the rest of us?" Ginny asked.

"Ho, ho, nope."

"Ya workin' tomorrow?" Tony questioned Shelly.

"Nah, I got to work the theater. We got a new movie. I always work the first couple showings of a new one. Just in case something goes wrong with it. They say I'm the best—"

"Mind if I come by?"

"No way, man. Not the first couple showings. The boss would have my ass."

"Hey, Tim, you play pool?" Jonny asked.

"Don't play with Jonny," Tom warned. "He's a shark."

"Don't mind if I do. I wield a pretty good cue myself."

Jonny smiled and started racking the balls, clicking them into the wooden triangle. "You want to break?"

"Sure." Tim was examining the house cues. He held one up so we could all see the curve. "What's this thing for?"

"Curve shots," came the instant reply.

Captain was going back to his drink. "That looks like Sal's prick," he said.

Sam started guffawing. "S-Sal's p-prick," he repeated.

"Hey, watch yourself or yous out of here. We got a lady present."

Captain didn't respond. He just slouched into his seat and made like he was planning a battle.

Tim searched through the cues. There weren't that many, but he took his time going over them a of couple times. Finally, he picked one. "You put money on the games?" he asked.

"If you insist," Jonny answered with a grin. We were grinning, too. Either way we were going to win. If Jonny won, well our house champ would have won and we'd have had the fun of watching him work his mark; Jonny would have sharked another patsy. Good entertainment.

If this new guy won, that would be fun, too. We were always hoping to see Jonny get his butt kicked. We could have gone over to O'Grady's and watch him play the real sharks, but that wouldn't have been the same deal.

We grabbed our drinks, gathered around, and settled in to watch.

Even Ephraim, carefully putting his guitar into its case, joined the circle. Sal, seeing that Ephraim wasn't going to play for a while, turned on that scratchy sound system of his. He turned up the volume until it became a blur of noise.

They settled on two bucks, enough for a drink. Straight pool. Twenty-five balls. "You wanna break?"

Tim's break shot may have been intended as careful, but he was well past the point of subtle physical control. *Jonny's going to run the table.* But he didn't, he was too good a hustler for that. Two balls, and then a third followed by the cue ball.

"Scratch," the would-be Santa exclaimed with unconcealed glee.

I could see Jonny licking his chops. He wanted this mark's money.

"Three ball in the side," Tim said indicating an easy bank shot.

"Bet ya can't."

"How much?"

"A buck."

"You're on." The shot was an easy one, even for an inebriated shooter.

"Nice," Jonny exclaimed as he handed over the dollar. He stood back and watched the new guy sink three more balls. "Maybe I've bitten off more than I can chew," he stage whispered to Chuck. "What do you think, Santa?"

"I think the guy's a magic elf," Shelly responded.

"Maaybee." Jonny scratched himself elaborately. "I don't know."

"Hey, quiet! This is a difficult shot." It didn't look that difficult, but if the guy wanted to play that way—"

"Who are you kidding?" For some reason I wanted to help Jonny pull it off. "What do you think, Jonny, can he make it?" As soon as the words were out, I realized that I was stepping on Chuck's turf. As the second best pool player among us regulars, it was his role to shill for Jonny.

"Nah, I got another buck that says no way."

"You're on." I was willing to part with a dollar knowing that Jonny would find a way to pay me back and would buy me a drink after the patsy had been fleeced. *Maybe I ought to give that drink to Chuck. Yeah, right!*

The ball thunked into the indicated pocket. It dropped through and ran along the gutter until it banged against the row of balls under the end of the table. Tim started looking for his next shot.

A miss, and it was Jonny's turn. He evened up the score. Then he picked a tough shot. There were plenty of easier ones on the table, but he obviously wanted to give Tim a little more line.

As he was indicating the shot with his cue, Jonny winked at me. I got the message. "No way, man."

"Want to lose another buck?"

I hesitated as if I were actually thinking about it. "What do you think, Santa," I asked, "Can he make it?"

"I don't know, he's pretty good," Shelly cut in.

Shit, doesn't he get it? "I meant the other Santa." I pointed at Tim.

"I don't know," this time the right guy answered. "He might."

"No way." I was emphatic. Meanwhile, I could feel Chuck's eyes burning holes in the back of my head.

Jonny blew the shot just like he'd planned. "Damn," he fake-mumbled under his breath as he handed me the same buck I'd given him.

Tim was feeling good. "Another drink," he called and rubbed his hands together in anticipation.

"Yous got the money?" Sal answered. He wasn't going to let this guy run a tab, not when Jonny was going to take him.

"Yeah, yeah." He went over to the bar holding a twenty in the air. "Here, just hang on to the change. I'm here to have a fun evening."

"Yes, sir," Sal said with dramatic emphasis and an honest grin. "Would yous like a fresh bowl of pretzels?"

Yeah, take 'em.

"Nah, I don't want nothin' on my hands while I'm playin'. This is a big game, there's money to be made."

Jonny grinned at me and chalked his stick.

"Jonny, yous want another one?"

"Nah, Sal, I'm good." We couldn't understand it, but we all admired the way Jonny would pace his drinking when he was playing pool. Of course, we knew that once all this guy's money was in his pocket that would be a different story.

"Enjoys yourself," Sal said as he handed the drink to Tim. "Oh, yeah, and Merry Christmas." This seemed to tickle Sal, wishing Santa Claus a merry Christmas; he started to laugh. Ginny joined in. Pretty soon we were all stupidly laughing and slapping one another on the back. It was definitely going to be a good evening.

The first game ended. Jonny made it look close, but he also made sure to win. With those two bucks in his pocket and all the bets on individual shots, he'd dropped only three or four overall. It was enough. Tim was obviously feeling sure of himself. The hook had been well set. "Give you a chance to win it back." Jonny suggested as he very deliberately put that bill into his breast pocket. It was one of his tricks—folding the bill so just a small portion of it peeked over the pocket edge, tempting even mocking the mark.

"Yeah, sure." I could almost see Tim's calculations. *I'm ahead, and this jerk thinks he won.* "But I think we should make it a little more sporting."

"What do you have in mind?"

"Five bucks for the game and three bucks for each ball."

"Okay …" Jonny tried to look like he was thinking hard. "What about scratches?" he asked.

"A buck?"

"Sounds fair."

"Fifty balls."

"Fifty?"

"Too many for you?" Jonny asked with a sneer.

"No, that's okay. It's I'm gonna be taking a lot of your money."

Jonny laughed. "Not if I can help it."

I turned to Chip and whispered, "Want to make a side bet?"

"Only if I get Jonny."

I laughed and took a swig of my drink. "No, I mean how much. I bet he takes this guy for a hundred."

"If he has a hundred."

"We'll find out." I winked at him. "How much do you think Jonny will get out of him?"

"I dunno."

Chuck pushed past us and gave me an elbow. "Sorry," I said acknowledging his anger.

"Yeah, sure." It came out clipped and nasty. Heads turned.

Just then Trish came into The Dew Drop trailing the drizzly wet behind her. "Hi, Trish," Ginny called out.

"What the fuck! What are we doing with all these Santas?" Trish took off her raincoat and draped it over a chair. "I haven't had anything to drink. I can't be seeing triple."

After getting her drink from Sal, she walked into the group of us gathered around the pool table. Playfully, she flipped each Santa's beard. "One of you the real deal?" she asked with a chuckle.

Tim let out a loud "Ho, ho, ho!" that set us all laughing and clinking glasses. Even Chuck relaxed.

"I'm the real one," Shelly announced. He, too, gave his best "Ho, ho, ho!"

"Uck," Ephraim reacted as Shelly's breath reached him.

"The hell you are," Chuck challenged.

"How about you, stranger?" Trish asked.

Tim looked at the other two. "I dunno; what do you think?" and another round of ho, ho, ho was the best he could muster.

"We got to figure out which of you guys is for real." Trish suddenly seemed really serious.

What ya got in mind?" Tony asked.

"How about a pool game?" Captain suddenly livening up suggested from his corner.

"What?" "That's dumb." "How would that—?"

"Great idea," Trish announced as if it were her decision.

Jonny had the clearest objection. "We're in the middle of a game here, Trish."

"Yeah, and they got a bet going." I added to back him up.

"You haven't even got the balls racked," Trish pointed out.

"The game can wait. We have an important question to settle," Captain announced as if he were giving an order. He marched over to the table and started racking the balls. "Chuck, Shelly, you boys choose your cues." He waited just a moment. "Okay, let's get lively here."

Jonny tried to say something, but Captain brushed him aside. "Official game to run here, Jonny. You can fleece Tim after we find out who's the real Santa." He bustled about as if they were readying a patrol into enemy territory.

In the process Captain was totally unaware of just how pissed Jonny was getting—and for good reason, there was real money involved. "That shithead," he muttered under his breath so only I could hear, "there's no way Chuck won't beat this patsy, and that will end my game."

"Yeah, I know."

"And he's already pissed at you for getting involved."

"Yeah." I sounded as contrite as I felt. I had gotten into the middle of their routine. Chuck was unquestionably pissed.

"Which means he's going to really beat this guy."

"Yeah." *What else can I say?*

The three Santas were standing by the table trying to decide the order.

"Lag for it," Jonny called over. When the Santas looked at him, he tried to wink at Chuck. "Just lag for it. Closest to the rail gets his choice."

It was a reasonable suggestion, which meant it only took a few more minutes of discussion to be adopted. Captain finally determined the order in which the three men tried their hand. As we expected, Chuck's ball came to rest closest to the rear bumper. Tim's was next. So it was Shelly who broke and Chuck who went second.

Before he lined up his first shot, Chuck glared at me and then looked at Jonny. Suddenly he smiled and shrugged his shoulders. *He's going to blow it.*

Sure enough, Chuck blew the easy shot that Shelly had left. It didn't matter what Shelly did; he'd never been able to sink a poll ball, and there was no reason to think he was about to suddenly learn how.

Captain had set the winning score, twenty balls. Tim won easily. Chuck, managing to do badly despite his natural competitiveness, ended with twelve. Shelly managed six.

Captain jumped up from his corner, walked up to Tim, and saluted. "You, sir, are the real Mr. Claus."

Tim grinned and saluted back. "Merry Christmas," he bellowed at his loudest.

There were congratulations all around. Ginny gave him a kiss, and Tim held his arms over his head and proclaimed "Ho, ho, ho!"

We took up a collection and bought him a drink. Then Chip offered a toast "to the real Santa Claus."

"To the real Santa," we echoed.

"Hey, Santa," I yelled even though I knew Chuck would resent it, "great game!"

Jonny went over and shook his hand. "I hope you're going to take it easy on me," he said with a wink that Tim could interpret one way while the rest of us knew what it meant.

A few minutes later they had started their game.

They played, but most of us weren't really paying attention. It seemed the entertainment value was gone. We were mostly disinterested.

"Hey, Ephraim, how about a song?" Tony suggested. "I wouldn't mind some decent music. Sal," he added, "you really need to get a TV for this dump."

"The Dew Drop ain't no dump," the barkeep answered.

"A dump? It sure is." Chip was quick to get involved.

"Watch yourself, or yous out of here."

"That's okay with me. I can go over The Oasis, at least they got a TV and a decent sound system."

In response, Sal cranked up the scratchy music, which made it even harder to hear.

I wanted to say something to Chuck, but he didn't look like he wanted to hear from me. So I watched him from across the room. He was sitting there looking unhappy and kind of bored. Tom went over and said something. Chuck nodded his head and looked like he might laugh, which made me feel a little better.

I edged closer just in time to hear Trish saying, "What happened to you? I know you play better than that."

"I didn't want to queer Jonny's game. He's gonna take that guy for everything he can."

"Oh." She sat down next to him. "That was real nice of you."

After a minute or two she said, "I guess that makes you the real Santa."

CHAPTER 22 - HAPPPY NEW YEAR

"G-god damn Ch-chink!" It was New Year's Eve day. Sam blasted into The Dew Drop. The chilly late afternoon wind followed him.

"Close the door," Sal yelled.

"What are you talking about?" I asked.

"That G-god-damned Ch-chink f-friend of yours. I went in to bu-buy an egg r-roll and he t-told me to g-get out of his r-restaurant. "

"Did you have money?"

"Yeah, yeah I had m-money." He put some cash on the bar. "Well, a d-drink'll be a better l-lunch anyway."

"So why did Chan throw you out? Come on, what did you do?"

"I d-didn't do nothin'. I j-just told him not to put no c-cat in it."

"Shit," I responded. "If I'd been working, I'd have helped him kick your butt out. What kind of dumb thing was that to say?"

"I was j-just joking."

"Dumb," I muttered.

"I h-heard that."

"Enjoys yourselves," Sal said. "No arguing here."

"Yeah, sure, Sal."

Sam slouched into the chair across from me. "How-how can you w-work for that g-guy?"

"Chan? He pays me okay and he gives me food. It's a good job. I mean it stinks and all, but I don't have any complaints."

"Well, I'd I'd have p-plenty."

"And he doesn't put cats in the food." I paused for a moment. "Or dogs neither. That's good Chinese. If you don't like it—"

"Wow, it's blowing out there." Ephraim came in. He'd been working delivering furniture. "I'm bushed."

He put a few bucks on the bar. "Can I buy you one?" he asked. It wasn't often that my buddy had any extra; but when he did, he was quick to buy.

"Yeah, s-sure."

"I wasn't asking you, Sam."

"Thanks."

Sal poured two and drew two beers. Ephraim brought them over and sat down next to me.

"W-what do you th-think of Chan?" Sam asked. No way would he drop an argument.

"His food or him personal?"

"B-both."

"Food's okay. I guess if you like Chinese. Him, I don't know. Who knows a Chinaman? Why are you asking?"

"He th-threw me out of his p-place today."

"Trying to get a free meal?"

"N-no. Why do you g-guys ..." He shrugged his shoulders and turned away.

"Hey, S-Sal, g-give me another one."

"Yous give me the money; I'll give yous the drink."

"J-Jesus," he muttered as he walked over to the bar. "You you all th-think I'm some k-kind of a m-mooch."

"I wonder why," I whispered to Ephraim who grinned in response.

Sam came back to the table. "I'm g-gonna sh-show him!"

"What?"

"Ch-Chan - I'm g-gonna g-get him. Tonight."

"What are you gonna do? I told you he's all right."

"Don't don't wor-worry, I'm just g-going to sc-scare him a little."

"Sam—" I started.

"I told you, don't wor-worry." He gulped down his drink, got up, and walked to the door. "I ain't g-gonna hurt him or nothing, j-just sh-ahoot off some Al-Albuquerque f-fireworks."

He was out the door before I could ask him what he meant.

"Albuquerque fireworks?" Ephraim asked.

I shrugged. "No idea. Sal?"

"Yous want a drink?"

"No, yeah, but what Sam said."

"Don't pay him no attention. That boy's about the flattest beer in the room."

We nursed our drinks and chatted about the day. One of the deliveries had been a whole living room set. "Fancy house. Some real nice paintings and stuff."

"What, were you casing it?"

For a moment Ephraim took my joke seriously. "Don't be stupid. I'm just saying, it was real nice. Good looking woman, too. Real fancy dresser. Reminded me of Sheila."

"Drop it!" I ordered.

"Look. I'm just saying."

"Well don't."

He didn't respond, just looked at his drink. Then, " Gave me a good tip."

"Oh."

"Said 'Happy New Year,' and gave each of us a twenty."

"Wow. No wonder you're buying."

"Yous playing tonight?" Sal had come over to the table and was standing next to Ephraim.

"I guess. Sure. I play every night, don't I?"

"Well it bein' New Year's. I just wanted to be sure."

"Why, we havin' a party?" I had to ask it.

"Yeah, jeez, I even bought an extra bag of pretzels."

"Ha, ha. The big time barkeep."

"I better get my guitar. Coming with me?"

"Sure." We finished our drinks. Just before we opened the door, I turned back to Sal. "What's that mean, Albuquerque fireworks?"

"Don't worry about it. Just bring that guitar … and some money … for the drinks."

"Hell, Sal, I thought you was treating us."

"Treating yous bums? That'll be the day."

"Not even one?" Ephraim tried.

"Get out of here. Yous guys. What a lousy way to earn a living."

***

Carol had brought a portable television to The Dew Drop. "So we can watch the ball drop," she explained. That was as close to a party as we got. We drank, ate the few pretzels Sal had put out, listened to Ephraim sing lots of lonely songs, and talked. We told a lot of stories we'd told before and mentioned people none of us wanted to see again but couldn't get out of our heads. Mostly, there was drinking.

It hit midnight local, and we all yelled "Happy New Year." There were a few hugs, a couple of kisses, and then Ephraim started to sing Auld Lang Syne, but he didn't know the words and no one else did either.

So we were all just humming along trying to make it sound like it mattered, when Sam came in. "You're kind of late," Chuck yelled to him.

"Hey, what happened?" Tony asked. "He's limping." he announced to the room.

"And trailing blood," Carol added.

"What the heck happened?"

"What did you do?"

"How did you...?"

Sam sat down at the table where Trish, Carol, Riley, and Greg were already sitting.

"Man, you need a doctor?" Riley asked.

"I d-donno. It h-hurts like h-hell."

Riley was looking at Sam's leg. "You've been shot."

"No fooling." The words came out simultaneously. I said it in surprise; Sam was being sarcastic.

"Damnedest gunshot I've every seen," Riley continued. Looks like the gun was aimed almost straight down. Was some asshole trying to make you dance?"

"You mean like the old Westerns?"

"Yeah, Greg, just like them old movies. Man, some people. I don't know."

Riley was prodding at the wound. "Ouch." Sam pushed the big man away. "T-that h-hurts."

"Who did it?" Even without tequila Chip was ready to beat somebody up.

We were crowded around waiting to hear a name or description. Sam mumbled something.

"What?"

"What did he say?"

"Who?"

Riley, who was closest to Sam, repeated, "He said nobody did it. He done it himself."

There was a moment of bedlam as we tried to make sense.

"I sh-shot my myself," Sam said clear and loud. "I d-didn't m-mean to. I was tryin' to s-scare those Ch-chinks. I'd t-told you I was shootin' off them Albuquerque f-fireworks, so I b-borrowed my c-cousin's g-gun, w-went over there, and s-started sh-shooting—you kn-know up in the the air.

"Next th-thing I kn-know my leg's on fu-fuckin' fire and bleeding and … I g-guess the bull-bullet came b-back down or ri-ri-ricocheted of something."

"You guess?" Greg said. "Sam, you're an idiot."

"M-maybe, b-but I bet I s-scared them out of their w-wits."

"Just where did you go?" I asked.

"Over to their r-restaurant. I-I bet I w-woke them out of a s-sound s-sleep."

I started to laugh. "What's so funny?" Ephraim asked.

"Chan don't live there. He lives over on the west of town."

"You been there?"

"Nope, but I seen pictures." I turned to Sam. "Nobody lives there you idiot. You shot yourself for nothing."

Sam was limping for weeks. Every time one of us saw him we'd start in laughing. I don't suppose he thought it was funny.

CHAPTER 23 - THE LETTER

When you don't hardly exist and no one cares, you don't expect, and usually don't want, letters. You figure they've got to bring bad news. Ephraim wasn't happy to see the envelope stuck in the door to his room. Gingerly, he pulled it out and turned it over and over in his hands.

"Mrs. Buthyre must have put it there," I commented, which was no help at all.

Finally, he focused on the front of the envelope and stared. I figured he was looking at the return address. "Who's it from?"

No answer. Instead he went into his room, put his guitar on the bed, and sat on one of those uncomfortable dinette chairs at the table.

I started to follow him into his room and then thought I might be intruding so I stood in the doorway and knocked on the frame. He looked up, surprised. "My mother."

"What?"

"It's from my mother."

"What does she want?"

"I haven't opened it yet."

"Ohhh … Yeah … You should … open it … I mean …"

He didn't say anything. Ephraim just stared at that envelope until I wanted to scream from frustration.

Finally, slowly, with careful fingers he opened it. Even more slowly he took the paper out and read it, carefully forming the words with his mouth.

It wasn't a long letter. He read it over and over. Each time mouthing the words. Making no sound.

Finally he looked up, realized I was still there, standing in the door. "She wants me to come to Des Moines."

Questions flooded my mind. I asked the only one that mattered. "You going?"

"I don't know. I have to … I guess I …" His voice drifted off.

"You want a drink?" What else could I say? I had half a bottle of some Four Roses hidden in my closet just in case and there were a couple of cans of beer left in the fridge.

He surprised me. "No, thanks. I think I'll ..." He went back to staring.

"Yeah, sure ..." I closed the door of his room and went to mine. There wasn't anything else to do about it, so I finished the Roses and the beer and smoked a few cigarettes. Finally, I fell asleep. That didn't do much good. I woke up in a shitty mood and with nothing to drink.

Eventually, I got it together enough to knock on Ephraim's door. He yelled to come in. There he was, still sitting at that table. The letter had been put down. He was holding his guitar—not like he was going to play it but like it was a girlfriend he was hugging for reassurance. I couldn't think of anything worth saying.

"What'd you decide?" I asked.

"I guess I gotta." There was sadness in Ephraim's eyes, something that said he might not make it. He kind of rocked back and forth, not like a crazy person but like a kid. Now that my big question had been answered, the little ones didn't seem important. I sat quiet, and I waited.

Finally a drop of information. "He's dead."

"Who?"

"Joshua?"

"Who?" I had no idea what Ephraim was talking about.

He stabbed at the letter. "The Mennonite. My mother's husband. Joshua. He's dead."

"Oh. How'd he ..." I dropped it knowing it didn't matter.

"She's got no one else."

"I thought she had a life there." It was a stupid thing to say, but I was angry, not just hung-over angry, but suddenly really pissed that my buddy was going to leave. *Who the hell does he think I have?*

"She needs me." So emphatic yet so filled with hurt.

I felt like a piece of crap—not just physically but in my heart. *I should be supportive. But ....*

"I have an idea." It was amazing how Ephraim's voice went from flat and pained to suddenly excited.

I stared at him—just looked in confusion until he continued.

"You come with me."

"What are you talking about?"

"Iowa. How far is it from Des Moines to Cedar Rapids, ten, twenty miles?"

"Farther than that."

"Okay, yeah, sure; but not that far. I mean it is the same damn state. Right?"

"Of course."

"So you've been talking about going to Cedar Rapid, right?" He didn't wait for a response. "We both go. You visit your folks. I go to be with my mom. Then once she's okay, you come live with us. It would be great."

If he'd only stopped rocking, I might have believed him; I might have gone along with the idea. He didn't. I didn't. I just kind of smiled and started thinking how dumb an idea it was.

"How are you gonna get there?" I changed the subject to something I knew. How many times had I studied the bus routes?

He looked confused. "I haven't thought about it. I spent all night just thinking about—"

"Well, I can help you with that. I mean the best route—"

"I hitched," he interrupted. I must have looked puzzled because he continued. "When I came here, I hitched from Des Moines."

"You can't go doing that now."

"Why not?"

I wanted to give him a speech about the times, and danger, and the seasons of the year and all those kinds of realistic things that seem important as you get older, but I knew I'd just be making them up. "'Cause your mom is counting on you. If something happens, who's gonna be there for her?"

"I guess—"

"You know I am. I've got some money saved, and you can—"

"I can't take the money you've saved up. That's for your—"

"For my nothing. I'm never going. Shit, I don't want to go. It's just a dream, a dumb one at that. Besides, I ain't giving it to you; it's a loan. You work in that bakery with your mom and save up, then you send me a check."

"Thanks." He sounded grateful and sad at the same time.

"Now don't you forget it's a loan."

"I won't."

***

On the way to Goodwill, we stopped at Frank's Spirits for breakfast. I bought a pint of vodka. Most of us liked Frank's because of his special policy for regulars: Buy a pint and get a free snack, beef jerky, pork rinds, pretzels—nothing big but salty and fatty. I got the pork rinds so we could share.

Ephraim surprised me. "I'm not drinking," he said and held the palm of his hand toward me as I offered the pint.

"Huh?"

"I decided last night, I'm on the wagon."

"Just like that?"

"No other way."

"You gonna go to meetings?"

"I don't know. Right now I don't need them. Later, in Des Moines, maybe. We'll see."

"You're serious."

"As serious as can be."

"Shitttt." I stood shocked, still for a moment. "Well, it's your call."

"You don't mind? I mean … You're okay if—"

"Not a problem." I took a gulp of vodka kind of to prove my point and tempt him at the same time.

It was at least a mile to Goodwill, but I said we should walk. It wasn't that we couldn't afford a bus. I had lots of money in my pocket, and I figured Ephraim probably had a few bucks, too. We could have taken a taxi if we could have found one in that part of town. I wanted to walk because I didn't want to rush the morning. I was hanging with my best friend, and it was gnawing at me that he was seriously talking about leaving. I was in no hurry.

By the time we sauntered into the Goodwill door, most of that pint and all the pork rinds were gone. "I don't want to get grease on everything," Ephraim said. It wouldn't have occurred to me, but he was right. So we hit the toilet first and washed up.

Ephraim looked real hard at himself in the mirror. "I'm not the kid I was."

"Who is?"

"Probably my brother." He brushed his hair back. It was long, light brown, and straight. His beard was a slightly different color—more red. His eyes were green, soft and caring.

Funny, I never really thought about it; he's a good-looking guy. "I guess you should get a haircut."

"Maybe I should wait and let my mother ..." He opened the door. "Let's get me some clothes."

The first item was a suitcase. Battered and stained, it was serviceable, something good enough for a one-way trip. Then came the clothes. We started with underwear and worked our way outward. Warm, serviceable, and not too ugly. Work boots and socks, a hat, gloves: the cart was filling.

"That should do it," Ephraim said.

"Wait a second," I responded. I had seen some really nice looking flannel shirts. "Let's get you a couple of these."

"I don't—"

"Don't be ridiculous; they'll look great on you." I held a couple out to him, and he took them—not reluctantly. While he tried them on, I pulled another shirt of the rack and tried it for myself.

We paid, folded everything we could into the suitcase and shoved the shoes and a heavy jacket into a paper bag. The one shirt I'd bought for myself was in a separate smaller bag tucked under my arm. We hopped a bus and headed for The Dew Drop.

"Where's your guitar?" Chip asked when we came in.

"We were out shopping."

"I can see that. What's the occasion?"

Ephraim talked about his mother's letter and about going to Des Moines.

"That's sweet," Trish commented. "It's nice that you and your mother ..." She stopped there, and we could all hear the catch in her throat.

"Let's have a party, a farewell party," Chuck suggested.

Everybody agreed. I wasn't sure how Ephraim felt about it, but he was willing. It had to be that night; he wanted to leave first thing in the morning.

I whispered to Chuck, "See if you can get the guys to throw in a few bucks. He doesn't have enough money to get there, and he won't let me give him anymore."

"Then how did he buy all that stuff?"

"He didn't, I paid for it. I've got some for his ticket, but not enough." I thought for a minute. "And I guess he'll need some food and cigarettes."

"And booze."

"He says no. He's giving up drinking. I guess he wants to be what he thinks his mother needs."

"He'll pick up."

"Probably, but not before he gets there."

"I'll ask around."

"Maybe Sal—"

"You got to be kidding."

"Yeah."

Come eight thirty that evening Sal surprised us both. "I really like the kid," was what he said. He'd sprung for some platters of sandwiches and even for a round of drinks. And he'd given Ephraim an envelope that held twenty bucks. Most of the others slipped him a five or a ten. Shelly handed him two tens, and Sharon added fifteen. There was more than enough for the bus to Des Moines.

"Thanks…thanks." That was all he could say, and it was enough.

Of course my friend had brought his guitar. He sang a lot, and we reminisced. Mostly we repeated ourselves and talked about Ephraim like he was dead or something. At some point it just seemed like we should quit. "One more song," Trish said. The suggestion was taken up by everyone.

"Sure." Ephraim started strumming. We sang that song people sing on New Year's, the one about Old Acquaintances. This time he remembered the words. I wondered, once he was in Des Moines, once he was with his mother, would my buddy remember me. Would he remember The Dew Drop?

***

The morning would come too soon. Ephraim and I stayed up most of the night just jawing away and remembering. I finished a couple of sixes, but he stayed sober, drinking Dr. Pepper, and telling me how he was going to start taking better care of himself.

I lied and told him I wished I had his willpower.

It's amazing how many things you can remember that aren't worth talking about. We remembered them all.

"What did that kid call you?"

"A bum drunk."

"What does that mean?"

"Damned if I know."

"I know." He looked pleased with himself. "Means you drink and stay fuckin' sober. No damned good at getting' drunk."

We laughed.

We laughed a lot that night. A couple of times I had to remind myself, *Don't start getting weepy.* Then I'd force myself to laugh. I figured Ephraim was doing the same.

About five we went to sleep.

Ephraim was knocking on my door well before eight. I dragged myself out of bed and got ready. The next bus to Dallas was at nine forty-five. *Damn, he could have let me sleep.*

"I want to get a good seat," he explained.

"How long you lay over in Dallas?" I asked already knowing the answer.

"Few hours." He looked kind of lost. "Then Saint Louis."

"Lay over there, too?"

"Of course. But that one goes straight to Des Moines."

"That's a long trip."

"You know you could still come."

"I don't think so."

"I mean straight to my mom's. You don't have to—"

Impulsively I hugged him. "I know. Thanks." I knew it was time. If we kept talking I'd probably get really bummed.

We grabbed a bus that dropped us off about a block from Greyhound. Ephraim had that suitcase, his guitar, and a large paper sack.

"You got everything?"

"I guess."

"If not, you write me."

"I'll write you either way."

We bought a couple of coffees at the stand. He bought a roll, took a bite, wrapped the rest in a napkin and stuck it in that paper bag. "I'll eat the rest on the bus."

"Sure."

An announcement about the bus to Dallas squawked over the loudspeakers. A line started forming, and Ephraim moved toward it. He looked back at me, and we shook hands the way guys do when they don't want to show the hurting.

I stood there for a few seconds staring after him. Then I figured I'd better leave. As I headed out of the terminal, I could have sworn I heard Ephraim calling me. I looked back, but he was talking to this black lady who was next to him in line. *Shit! I need a drink.* I headed down the street. *How long before Sal opens?*

CHAPTER TWENTY FOUR - GENUINE PEARLS

"Wow!" I had never seen Trish dressed up. She usually looked one step from being a bag lady. *Where did she get those clothes?* It was a blue suit and pastel pink blouse. Black high heels and a choker of pearls. Her hair had been done—still gray but nicely in place. Her fingernails and lipstick matched with enough mascara and shadow to make her look like a wealthy matron.

"Is that you, Trish?" I shook my head like I was trying to clear my eyes. "You look great."

She smiled.

"Quite the change, isn't it?" Sharon was smiling, too.

"Did you help her?"

"No, well I helped pick the lipstick."

"And apply the makeup," Trish added. "Sharon was a dear."

"How come?"

She crossed The Dew Drop and settled into the chair next to Carol.

"Are those real?" Tony asked pointing to her pearls.

"A gift from my husband. Years ago." Her voice trailed off.

"They're beautiful," Carol commented. "May I?" She touched them gently.

"Yous want a drink?"

Trish started to say yes. Then stopping herself, "Do you have a white wine?" I couldn't imagine what Sal might have on hand or how long it might have sat in a half-emptied bottle.

"A cardonny."

"What?" Sharon looked at him in horror.

He spelled the word "C H A R D O N N A Y"

"That's a Chardonnay."

"Excuse me, I don't sell much wine in here."

"How long has it been sitting there open?" Sharon demanded.

"I got no idea. When was the last time one of you bums ordered a glass of white wine?"

We looked around at one another as if it was a question that could be answered. Tony interrupted the silence, "A long time."

"Yeah," Sal echoed, "a long time."

"Maybe I'd better just have a beer." Trish tried to make it sound like she was doing him a favor.

"Sure, a shot with that?"

"No, just the beer."

He handed the glass to Tony who brought it to Trish. She handed him a bill, "Thank you, my good man." She tried for a snooty accent.

Tony guffawed. "Boy, ain't you got airs."

"Leave her alone." Sharon's voice was loud and sharp.

"Wish my customers acted like that, you know polite and everything," Carol said.

"Well, I ain't …" Tony didn't bother finishing.

"What gives?" I tried again.

"My daughter is coming … for my birthday."

"Your daughter?" Chuck sounded as surprised as I felt. "You got a daughter?"

"A daughter and a son. He doesn't want—" She stopped in discomfort. "She's coming for my birthday."

"How old are you?"

Tony kicked Chip. "You ain't supposed to ask no lady how old she is."

"Trish ain't—" Chip started again. "She's family. It ain't the same thing."

Trish said, "I don't mind. I'm turning seventy."

"Seventy. Wow! You don't look a day over fifty." Greg was being polite. Ordinarily Trish looked old and used beyond recovery. Ordinarily, I would have guessed her to be at least eighty. Even dressed up, the creases in her face, the thinning of her hair, and the liver spots on her shaking emaciated hands made her look old.

"So you have two kids?" I tried to change the subject. "Any grandkids?"

"My daughter has two children. They live with their father." There was an uncomfortable silence. "My son has one little girl—at least that I know of." She choked for a moment. "He …" She started over. "I don't hear from him. Sophia, my daughter, talks to him, not often, but they talk, so I hear some from her. I understand he's doing really well. He sells computers."

Now she was talking freely like a valve had been turned. "The little girl's name is Mary. She's seven." Trish started to cry. "I've never met her. He did send me a picture. One. Mary was just a baby." From her purse she pulled out a birth announcement with an infant's photograph printed on it.

"Sophia sends me pictures." She pulled a photo of a boy and girl posing with Santa Claus. "Aren't they adorable? This is from last Christmas."

She passed the photos around, and we all made appropriate comments that meant nothing. "They look like nice kids," I said hardly looking at the picture.

"They're beautiful," Carol corrected me drawing out the word.

"Is Sophia bringing the children?" Sharon asked.

"She doesn't have them."

"Yeah, you said they lived with their father," Tony reminded us all.

"How come?" Tom was right to the point.

"Sophia had problems."

"Drinking?" Tom asked.

"No. Depression. She was in the hospital, and he ... he filed for divorce while she ... shock treatments and everything, and he ..."

"Another beer, Sal." She had gulped down the last one with a bitter grimace.

"That's tough," Sharon commiserated. We all agreed.

"At least he lets her see them."

I sat for a moment, uncomfortably, remembering my own family.

Jonny came in. He looked around. "Boy, what a party. You guys look like you're at a funeral."

"Yeah, and today's Trish's boithday," Sal said.

"No, tomorrow," she corrected him. "But my daughter's coming today."

"No wonder you're all dolled up." He unzipped his pool cue case, pulled out the pieces and screwed them together. "You gonna celebrate?"

"I thought I might take her out for dinner. Someplace quiet so's we can talk."

"When was the last time?" Chip asked.

"On the phone, last week when she told me ..."

"No, I meant when you saw her."

"Five, six years. Like I said, she's had a tough time."

"I got to ask yous something," Sal put in. "Yous taking her to dinner, and yous all dressed up; how are you doin' it?"

I had been wondering the same thing, but I'd been embarrassed to ask.

"What do you mean?"

"The money." Sal didn't hesitate, especially about money. "Yous never seem to have nothin'. Where ya getting' the money?"

Trish laughed bitterly. "Oh, I've got money. Not a lot, but enough. My husband was an engineer."

"Which railroad?" Riley asked.

"Not that kind. He designed stuff, made it work—electrical stuff like computer stuff. He made a good living, and he left me some. Then I get my Social Security. I got money, I just don't have my family." She finished off the glass of beer in front of her and looked imploringly at Sal.

"Yous want another?"

Trish nodded.

"You really shouldn't," Sharon said.

"I need it."

"At least you can help your kids out," Tony said.

"Kevin doesn't need it. I'd help Sophia, but she's never—"

"Asked?" I tried to finish for her. She nodded her assent.

"It's nice she's coming for your birthday," Greg suggested.

"I guess. I hope." She shook her head in a kind of dejected way. "I just don't ..."

***

"What the devil?" Sal was pushing the back door of The Dew Drop, but it wouldn't open—not all the way. "I got ta get last night's garbage out to the dumpster before they pick up."

"Something must be blocking it." Chip said. "Some kids must have been out there last night."

Sal had just opened, and we had piled in behind him.

"One a yous go 'round and see what's in the way," Sal asked.

"Sure," Tony and I said at the same time.

For some reason, Ginny found this very funny. "The new Siamese twins 'll go," she said between laughs.

"I don't think that's so funny," I commented angrily.

"Take it easy," Sal scolded.

"You know we all miss him," Jonny put it.

"Yeah, 'specially when Sal plays that music of his." Riley's comment gave us all something to grin about.

"Yous don't like my music, then don't send the guitar player to no Des Moines."

Yeah, that was it. I was missing my buddy. I might like Tony, or Chip, or any of the other guys; but none of them were going to replace Ephraim.

"How about that door," Ginny reminded us.

We went out the front, turned left, went to the alley, another left, and back around the building.

"Holy shit!" Tony was in front of me, so he saw her first.

Trish lay on the ground. There was blood, not a lot just enough to add to my upset.

"Looks like she bumped her head."

I banged on the door. Sal pushed against it, but I kept it from hitting Trish's body. "Call the cops and EMS," I shouted.

"What's —"

"Trish. She's out here! She's lying on the ground."

"Is she ...?"

"I don't know. Tony?"

"I think she's breathing, but not—"

"Move her out of the way. I'm coming out."

Ginny's voice was commanding. Without thinking, Tony and I dragged Trish away from the door so the others could reach us.

"Come on, Trish, hang in there." Ginny crouched by her head and was stroking her hair. It was no longer done up and was sticky with blood.

"Did you call the paramedics?"

"Yeah, yeah, I'm getting them now."

"Is she…?"

"We should carry her inside." We did as Ginny instructed. Later they told us it didn't matter, but we shouldn't have. Anyway, we did. Everybody except Riley. He was looking down. Trish's string of pearls had broken, and the little white balls were everywhere. Slowly, the big black man bent down and picked them up, one by one.

By the time the police and the ambulance had arrived, he had gathered as many as he could find. He held them in one giant hand wandering from one of us to the next asking, "What should I do with these?"

No one had an answer.

***

Trish was not dead—not yet. She lived out that day, her birthday. She died the next, not having regained consciousness. The hospital said she died of a heart attack. "Probably hit her head when she fell," the social worker who eventually answered our inquiries explained. "Lost some blood, but that didn't do any real harm."

We had no idea what to do. She had stuff, an apartment, a body—yes, a body that needed doing with. We had no authority.

Sharon had a key to Trish's place. She and Ginny went over and looked for whatever they could find. There wasn't much. They did find her daughter's phone number. Nobody answered. Not call after call.

There was a nasty letter from her son. It had a return address. They wrote. The letter came back. Trish belonged to the city and the county. That was a sad and very final end.

There was another letter. Chuck had it. He had seen Trish that night. She had been staggering drunk; wandering the streets and moaning like a child.

"You're the real Santa Claus, aren't you?" she had asked him.

"I didn't know what to say," he told us. "I'd never seen her so bad.

"Anyway, she hands me this letter and says, 'I've been a bad girl, Santa. Here's my letter.' Then she kind of pushed me away. I wanted to help her, get her home, bring her here, but she just pushed me away and went wandering off.

"I wish …"

He handed Sal an envelope. Ginny grabbed it away. "It just says 'Mother'." She turned the envelope over and over.

"Will you open it, or else give it to me," Sharon demanded.

Slowly, reluctantly, Ginny lifted the flap. She read for a moment. Tears. Sniffing. She handed it to Sharon, who also read in silence.

Sharon took a gulp of air and a healthy sip of her drink. "Mother," she began.

"I cannot have dinner with you. I do not want to. I have not come to Albuquerque to celebrate your birthday. I wish you had never been born. If you had not, then neither would I. That would have been better.

"Jack's new wife doesn't want me around the children, my children. He is supporting her. They've gone to court. My lawyer says I'll win, that he can't do that to me. But I know he can. One way or another. Without my children I might as well be dead; I am dead.

"Is it all your fault? I don't know. Maybe if you hadn't been a drunk. Maybe if you … Oh, I don't know. I just know that I hate you, and I hate me even more.

"So I'm going to leave this letter at the restaurant and go back to Austin. I'm not sure if I will kill Jack, Marjorie, or myself. Maybe I'll just start drinking like my mother.

"Goodbye, Sophia"

There was a long pause. We drank and smoked, and said little.

"She must have needed a drink." Chip eventually commented.

"I don't think so." Sharon's voice seemed almost reedy, reluctant. "I think she needed something more."

"Much more," Ginny added.

"What?" Tony asked.

"To be home," I answered.

"To be with family," Greg said.

"Oh."

There was another long silence. More drinks. More cigarettes.

"What should I do with these?" Riley asked. He had reached into his pocket and pulled out a plastic baggie; it held the pearls he had gathered and had carried with him since.

Nobody had an answer.

"Maybe I should throw them in the dumpster?"

"Nah, they's worth money." Leave it to Sal.

"Yeah, we could sell 'em and have a party … like a wake for Trish." Chip suggested.

"I have a better idea," Ginny said. "You still see that girl?" she asked Riley.

"What girl?"

"The girl with the green hair."

"Gladys. Yeah, I see her time to time. Why?"

"You should give 'em to her."

The reactions were immediate. "You're crazy." "Carlton would cut off her tits." "What would she …?"

Riley looked at Greg, who nodded back. "Ya know, that ain't a bad idea. I'll give them to her, and who knows …"

The thought hung in the air.

CHAPTER 25 - WANTED

"Cops are looking for you," Ginny informed me as soon as I got to The Dew Drop that day.

"How come?"

"How would I know? They were asking where you were."

"What did you tell them?"

"That this is the best place. Maybe the Chinese place."

"Shit, Chan'll have a fit; he's afraid of the cops."

"Y-yeah, if-if they ever f-found out w-what he was serving." Sam still had his thing about the Chinese.

"What did yous do?"

"Oh, yeah, I told them to check the deli," Ginny said at the same moment.

"Why?" I whined.

"What did yous do?" Sal asked again, louder.

"Nothing. I didn't do nothing." I couldn't believe he'd even ask. "Couldn't you have just told them you'd tell me?"

Ginny looked stricken. "I'm sorry. I tried to tell them you'd come by the precinct, but they weren't having it." With a shrug she added, "You know what cops are like."

Sal was knotting a bar towel in his hands. Clearly he didn't like his girlfriend getting upset.

"Couldn't you have …?" I didn't know how to finish the question.

"Oh, hell, give me a drink." I figured I'd have a quick one and then call the cops. No sense waiting for the bad news, whatever it was. I didn't have time to finish before two uniforms showed up, a man and a woman, grabbed me, and shoved me against the bar.

"Hey …"

"Shut up." He twisted my arms behind my back pulling them harder than he needed. Once the cuffs were on, she patted me down.

"I don't …"

"Ooww," I howled as she squeezed my privates.

"Keep that mouth shut," she growled.

"Yes, ma'am," I answered hoping to placate.

She gave another squeeze, "I said shut."

I moaned in painful acquiescence.

As they marched me out of The Dew Drop, she was reading that dumb card telling me I had the right to keep silent—like I was going to try to open my mouth again.

The room they stuck me in reminded me of a cage at the zoo. I was forced onto a hard metal chair. My left wrist handcuffed to a matching shiny table. I had to piss, and my legs were jiggling from that and anxiety. Worse, I was alone, not knowing what was going to happen. *When do they bring in the lions?*

The door opened. Two angry looking guys walked in. "My name's Brown, and he's Swanson," one of them said in a bass voice. "Now what the hell were you thinking of?"

I looked at him as blankly as my mind felt. "I got to piss."

"Who cares?" Swanson asked. His voice was higher, but it had a tinge of nastiness that made it much scarier than Brown's.

"What kind of asshole are you?"

"I have to go bad."

One of them kicked the chair from under me. My ass hit the floor; the handcuffed wrist yanked my shoulder. "Ohhh!" I cried. I could feel the wet of urine flowing.

"Get up, and sit in that chair." Swanson sounded like he was enjoying himself.

I managed to get up. My shoulder felt like my arm had been pulled off. Tears were starting down my face.

"You piece of shit, did you piss yourself."

Yeah, he's having fun. The bastard.

I sat in the chair feeling the wet and clamminess of my pee and wishing I were somewhere, anywhere else.

"Did you really think you could get away with it?"

"I don't know what you're talking about." It was the truth, and I knew the two cops wouldn't believe it.

One of them whacked the back of my head. "Why don't we make this easy?"

I grunted.

"Start talking, or it's gonna get rough." Brown straddled the chair opposite me.

"I don't—"

Swanson's hand thumping the back of my head stopped me. "None of that 'I don't know' crap," he stage whispered in my ear.

"Craig, Craig, let the shithead speak before you whack him." Brown seemed to smile at me; it was more of a leer. "Now you tell us about Beck and Beck."

What the hell's he talking about? "I worked there for a while,"

"That's better." He turned to his partner. "Craig, I think our friend here wants to help us." He got right into my face. "You want to help us, don't you?"

I nodded.

He reached over and patted my left hand like he was trying to reassure me. Then he grabbed it and squeezed. "I'm sure you don't want to waste our time."

The pain of his squeezing was nothing compared to the pain I had already suffered, but he had honed his point. I nodded again with more intensity. "I want to help," I squeaked.

"So you worked at Beck and Beck?" he continued. "Tell us the rest of the story."

Do they know about Sheila? Do I want to tell them? Will they ... I was lost.

Another whack on the back of my head got me talking. I told them about Sheila, about the sex, about the fire escape, about her brother, about it all. They laughed. "That squares with her diary. At least most of it. Nothing about her brother ..."

"Steven," I provided.

"Yeah, Steven." Brown laughed a nasty chuckle.

"She says you were pretty pathetic in bed." Swanson used a nasty stage whisper. "I guess she wanted somebody she could look down on."

"A tiny prick, too." Brown looked at me. "Well, you showed her."

Embarrassed, confused, I focused on my wet underwear. It felt cold, and I felt stupid. I remembered church on Sunday morning in Cedar Rapids. I must have been about six. Mom had told us to go to the bathroom before we left for church, but I hadn't needed to go then. Sitting in the hard pew with nothing to distract me, I had started to squirm in need. My father had hit me on the back of the head and told me to keep still. I tried, and I tried to hold back the urine that was demanding release.

"I have to go to the bathroom," I finally whispered.

"Your mother told you to go at home. Now, sit still." He sounded angry, like he was ready to hit me. I said no more. Instead, I surrendered. I had lost the battle. My pee soaked me and leaked onto the seat of the pew. My parents could smell it. They could feel it trying to soak through their clothes as well. My father grabbed me and dragged me from the church while my mother desperately used his and her handkerchiefs to clean my flood. Then she, too, Jan in tow, had left the service.

The two cops had stopped laughing. "So you admit you knew her?"

"I told you."

"You loved her?"

"I made love to her. It isn't the same. I don't know why she ... I liked her. But when I realized ... I mean would you ..." I stammered about and knew I wasn't making them happy. Finally, I managed, "What ... why are you asking ... what is this about?"

Another whack.

"I'm trying—"

Whack. "Shut up."

I sat my head down. Brown opened the door. He was talking with somebody who handed him a clear plastic bag. He put the bag on the table. In it was the envelope from my drawer, the one with my Cedar Rapids money and the lighter Sheila had given me.

"Guess what we found in your room."

"That's my money. I saved it."

"A bum like you! How'd you save nearly a hundred bucks?"

"There was a hundred and seven and some change. Did somebody steal—"

So you admit you had it?"

"I told you it's mine."

"And this lighter, too. That's yours?"

"Yeah."

"Your name's Sheila, huh? Boy, are you stupid, keeping that. Your ass is fried."

"I didn't. I swear ... It was a—"

I landed on the floor again.

Looking up at the two of them grinning and Swanson getting ready to kick, I managed to find the courage. "I want a lawyer."

That didn't stop the kick.

"I want a lawyer." This time I screamed.

The next time I sobbed it.

Brown said, "Screw you," and gave me a final kick. Then they left.

I must have passed out. I woke in a cell. There were three other guys in there. There were a couple of bunks. You'd have thought somebody would have tossed me on one of them, but they hadn't. I was on the floor, stuck in a corner. At least nobody had stolen my shoes or knifed me for the fun of it. They just stared at me like I was supposed to be the entertainment.

"Hey, he's awake," one of my cellmates said.

They all stared harder. Another asked, "Man, you know you stink?"

"Leave him alone. He ain't the first guy to piss himself."

"Or shit himself neither."

Great. They know. I tried to get up. One of the guys, the one who had asked about stinking, helped me to my feet.

"We'd of put you on a bunk, but we were afraid to move you. The way the pigs threw you in here, we figured you might not make it."

"They went to town on you, fella."

"Yeah, you've been lying here about eight hours."

"Ten," another one corrected. "Lying and moaning in your sleep."

I nodded.

"What'd you do?"

"I'm not sure."

"They didn't tell you?"

"No. They were asking me about this place I'd worked a while, Beck and Beck; they sell business supplies?"

"Shit, they think you done that?"

"Done what?" Before he could answer, "I got to take a crap."

They pointed to a seatless bowl in the corner of the cell.

I sat there, feeling naked and vulnerable and wishing I was anywhere while they talked about the break-in at Beck and Beck.

"She must of surprised whoever it was. I hear he used a hammer on her."

"I heard a knife."

"No, her head was smashed in. No knife."

"Who?" I asked even though it drew attention to me. "Who are you talking about?"

"The girl who got killed. I think she was the manager."

Sheila, shit no, the cops must...

"So they think you done that?"

"I guess." *Oh, my God, why do they... What the hell do I ...* There was nothing but confusion.

I wiped myself with the sandpaper that was next to the toilet and washed my hands. "A towel?" I asked holding my hands up and feeling foolish.

"Use your clothes."

"Or some of the terlit paper, or what they call terlit paper."

I pulled some of the rough paper. "Hey, not too much. They won't give us no more till tomorrow."

"I didn't do anything. I won't be here that long," I said even as I rolled some of the paper back."

"Oh, you'll be here."

"Not once my lawyer—"

Their laughter cut me off.

"Yeah, Legal Aide. Right? Your Legal Aide lawyer, who won't be worth shit, will meet you about two minutes before you're arraigned. Then, if you're lucky, you'll see the son-of-a-bitch before they offer you a plea. In your case it'll probably mean life."

"I told you—"

"Yeah, we know, you didn't do it. You know what that's worth? Squat!"

I sat down on the wooden bench against one side of the cell. Behind it was a gray cement wall. It felt as if the wall was falling on me.

Two of the others were sitting on the bench. The third guy was lying on one of the bunks and smiling a thin crazy smile. "We're all guilty," he said. "Maybe not doin' what the cops say, but doin'."

"What did you do?" I asked.

"I ain't tellin' that, but they say I was exposin' myself."

"Tell the truth or shut up," one of the others said. "You don't think we already know."

The other guy, who looked like a bear or something, growled as how he'd heard more than enough already.

"Okay," the guy on the bed said. "It doesn't matter what anyone does so why not." He crossed himself like he was in church confessing. "I grabbed this kid and took her into the bathroom at the park. I was gonna' sex her, but somebody'd seen. You satisfied?"

"Did you?"

"I never got a chance."

"Must of scared the shit out of that kid."

"I don't know. Some homeless kid. Didn't say nothing. Probably use to it. What's the big deal? Not like it matters. She'll end up selling it to someone."

My mind flashed. *Was it Darlene? That poor kid.* I visualized reticent Lucile and her three kids. *Are they making it? Are they still getting those cans?*

"You piece of shit." One of the other guys shouted as they both stood up and moved toward the molester. He curled up like he was expecting a beating, maybe like he'd asked for it.

They grabbed him and started punching. I wanted to join in, but couldn't quite get myself moving.

He may have wanted the pounding, but the guy still screamed in pain.

"Shut up in there, or I'm bustin' some heads."

The three of us glared. The blows stopped. The guy on the bed yelled, repeating, "We're all guilty.We're all guilty.We're all guilty."

I could hear my father in his voice. *What did I do? What do they think I did?* I shrank inside myself and waited.

A cop looked into the cell. "Quiet it down. You hear me?"

The other guys sat back down.

Another whimpered, "We're all guilty." Then just gasps.

"You fucking pieces of crud," the cop said. "No more of that in here. Wait till you're over at county."

***

"No bail." The judge banged his gavel, and that was that. It wouldn't have mattered if he had set bail. I didn't have any money. Even my lousy hundred bucks was locked up at the property desk. My legal aide attorney, Sawyer, who didn't remember me, wasn't interested in anything I had to say. "Just tell him not guilty, and we'll worry about strategy later on," he said.

"But I didn't—"

"That's fine," he interrupted. "Now, do what I said."

From court I was taken to the county lockup. I hoped it would be better than the police station where I'd spent the night. It was and it wasn't.

I had a shower. I got clean clothes—an orange jumpsuit, and a halfway decent meal: chili, heavy on the beans and the farting, and thick-crusted bread, even some canned peaches. Then they stuck me in a cell with this quiet guy. Frank was waiting for trial, too. He said he had found his girlfriend turning a trick and assaulted the john. "What would you have done?" he asked.

"I guess the same," I answered not wanting to make an enemy.

"Right on," Frank said giving me a fist bump. "I'd do it again." He was quiet for a couple of minutes. "Of course now I wouldn't bother with her, not knowing."

"Shit, who am I kidding? I'm still hot for her."

That part was all good. If I had to be locked up, I couldn't do much better than a good guy like Frank.

The bad started about three o'clock that afternoon; that's when the horror began.

Never having cold-turkeyed before, I didn't know what to expect—not the bugs crawling my body, not the sense of terror, not the seizing motion of my body, and not the screaming dreadfulness of my thoughts. The guards dragged me to the infirmary where someone gave me a shot. Later, once again awake, I sweated and screamed—helplessly restrained and terror stricken. I begged for something, anything to help: a pill, a shot, or best of all a drink. The staff ignored me, the trustees told me to shut up. That I wasn't the first guy to go through detox there and I wasn't going to be the last.

I puked a couple of times. Lying in vomit did nothing to help. I wanted to die, and I was afraid that I was dying. It seemed to last for days, weeks. Time stood still; only the racking of my body had dimension.

Eventually, starting to feel better, I was actually hungry. At first they wouldn't feed me, just sips of water. When I did finally eat, I started heaving. Nothing came up, which was worse than if it had.

"I must have eaten something," I said to one of the trustees.

He laughed. "I must have et the same thing before they locked me up." He had a damp sponge and wiped off my face and chest. "It'll get better," he said, "just take it easy."

Take it easy. Yeah, sure. I wish I had a drink, just enough to get me by. Something to turn it off. If I don't get a belt, I'm gonna die. I wish I were dead. Yeah, that would be...

I drifted in and out of consciousness, life, delirium, sleep. Eventually it was over. The D.T.s had ended. I was dry, but I still wanted a drink. I would have killed for a beer. At least my body was no longer alien territory.

Back in a cell with another cellmate. Damond.

He was a nasty sucker doing twelve-years for armed robbery and back in town for a trial. "Don't bother me, and I won't mess with you," was his introductory comment. Damond didn't keep his word; he messed with me plenty—just pushing me around because he could.

"You're lucky," he said.

"Why?"

"'Cause I don't like ass." He pushed me against the bars. "And your mouth ain't big enough for my pecker."

God, I want a drink.

A couple of the guys from The Dew Drop visited me. Others had tried before, while I was still in the infirmary. "Greg, is there anything you guys can do to help?" I asked. "Maybe Sal could."

Tony shook his head and told me it sucked—like I didn't already know that. Greg said something about trusting in the Lord, which helped even less. They gave me a thumb's up as they went and left me feeling even worse.

"You got a visitor," one of the guards told me.

"Who?" Figuring he didn't know or care, but I wanted to say something, anything, just to sound like a human and not a caged animal.

"Some reporter," he answered. "She wants to do a story on you. Let me give you some friendly advice."

"Yeah?" We were walking down the tier. Some new guy was screaming. The sound filled me with nausea. "Jesus," I muttered. *Did I sound like that?*

The guard ignored the noise. "Don't make trouble."

"What?"

He turned to face me and smiled—it was a nasty look. "You heard me, don't make trouble. No phony complaints, no 'you got to investigate this' or 'you should do a story about that.' Understand?"

"I got no complaints … except maybe that I'd love a beer."

"You just keep it that way." He pushed me through the door into the visiting area—tables with fixed seats and nothing that could be thrown. Men and women in orange jumpsuits; their visitors, mostly dark-skinned and looking poor.

I stood there glancing around and thinking it was a mistake. Then I saw her—Monica. But her real name was something different; I couldn't remember what. She waved to me. I walked over and sat down.

"You mind if I take notes?"

"Why are you here?"

"To do a story."

"About what?" I asked feeling stupid. "You planning to make a fool of me again?"

"About you. You're a big-time felon." She looked at me. "I must admit that's hard to believe. But you might be good copy. That other thing was just for fun, but this story... This is big."

"I didn't do it." I started to tear up and then to cry straight out. I hated that moment, but I felt release—like a little kid who's hoping his mommy will somehow take care of a problem, a problem that just seems too big to even understand. "I swear to you, Monica, I didn't."

"That's not my name, and that's not what I came hoping to hear."

"What did you want me to say?" I choked out the words.

"First off I want you to call me Muriel."

"Fine, Muriel, I swear I didn't—"

"Next," she interrupted, "I want a story that will grab people: how you went bad, how you screwed up your life, why you broke into that store, why you raped her, why you killed her. I want the whole thing."

Suddenly nothing made sense. "Rape? Sheila?" I gasped the name. "Sheila?" I repeated it. "Did somebody…?" I couldn't quite wrap my head around it. "They think I raped Sheila. No, no. Monica. Sorry I mean Muriel, I didn't. Oh, my God, rape. I knew there was a robbery, but rape."

I couldn't hold back the tears.

"Yeah, that's what they figure. You broke in to rob the place. You knew how 'cause you had worked there. She was working late, and you lost it. They say you and she had had something going. Did you?"

I told her about Sheila, about how I'd met her, how she'd climb the fire escape, about her brother. I told her everything I'd told the cops and more. I ended by repeating, "I didn't do it."

"No wonder they like you for it."

"I didn't, I swear it, Muriel, I swear." I started to say it again. I didn't know what else to say. Then, helpless, I stopped.

"So what's your alibi?"

"I don't know."

"You don't know? That helps a lot."

"I mean, I don't know when she … when the robbery. They never told me."

Looking in her notebook to be sure, Muriel gave me the time and date. I looked blank. *How the hell would I know?* "It's hard to say," I said. "It's not like I have this schedule, like I keep a diary or anything. Where the hell was I?

"I know where I wasn't. I wasn't at Beck and Beck. Why would I go there? I never —"

"Where do you go nights?" she asked. I figured she already knew the answer.

"Most nights I go to The Dew Drop. Then I go back to my place. That is unless I'm working at Heinrich's or The Shady Rest. Some nights I work those places—you know, cleaning up.

"I used to work nights at Beck and Beck, but I guess that doesn't help. That was a while ago and the cops already know … Like I said, some nights I work at the nursing home; that's Sundays. And the deli; there different nights but almost always on Thursdays unless it's a holiday. They get real busy Fridays, so they like to have the place cleaned up Thursdays."

For the moment I had hope, and that made me talk.

Muriel was looking at her calendar. "Shit, that was a Thursday," she said. "It was a god-damned Thursday. This could be big." She sounded excited. "You may have a god-damned alibi."

"So you'll go talk to them? Maybe they'll have a record or something."

"On one condition."

"What?"

"I'm the only reporter you talk to."

"You're the only reporter I know."

"I won't be, not if you go to trial."

"But if Heinrich—"

"That'll be up to the D.A. Do we have a deal?"

"Yes, hell yes. I promise. You're the only one. Just, please, please, go ask them. Maybe I'll …" There wasn't anything else to say.

"Once again the police have arrested the wrong man. Once again they have failed to check out an alibi." That was how her story began. It didn't say much about me; who the heck would want to read about a loser? Instead there was a lot about courageous reporting and the importance of community oriented policing. And there was some stuff about how the Beck siblings had put their family business up for sale, how they couldn't cope with going to that store and thinking about their dead friend and employee.

The chief of police wouldn't comment. He sent two detectives, different detectives, to interview Magda and Heinrich. Magda did the talking.

The cops asked how she knew I'd worked that night. "I keep records," she'd answered just as she had to Muriel. "I keep good records. He worked Thursdays, almost always on Thursdays."

"Sure, but how do you know he didn't leave and come back?"

"You don't think we have camera? He couldn't do that. I'm not so dumb as to take his word. I liked him; he never stole beer, sometimes a sandwich or some salad, but no beer. Still I made sure. I had my camera. No, he was here in the store. I can show you." She had riffled through a box of old surveillance tapes until she found that night and gave it to them.

"Do I get it back?" she asked.

"Why? Do you need it?" One of the detectives asked.

"I keep them. You never know. I kept this one, and now you need it."

Her husband said little except to tell them that his wife was never wrong.

"Never?"

"Not about business. That's why we make a profit." With that he had gone back to slicing meats for a catering order.

The detectives had taken careful notes.

***

Twelve days had passed. I was free. I'd lost my jobs. "We had to find somebody else," Heinrich explained.

"You no show up," Chan told me with inscrutable logic.

My stuff was in the basement. Mrs. Buthyre was looking for a new tenant. "You owe me for two weeks already," in a tone that said it was all my fault and that she didn't want me back—not a known felon.

I tried talking to the police, asking for help. I went to headquarters, not sure what they could do, but hoping for something. The receptionist let me sit for a while. When I didn't leave, she sent me to a community affairs representative, who looked like she couldn't care less.

I explained the situation. "Maybe you could send a cop to talk with them," I pleaded. "I don't have any job or anyplace to live. It isn't fair; my life's upside down, and I didn't do anything wrong. If those detectives had checked out my alibi … If they'd even found out I had one …"

The woman clucked a few times in what I thought was sympathy; then said, "You got a complaint, hire a lawyer and sue us."

"But those cops—" I started.

"Not my problem."

I tried again, "I don't want to—"

"You can file a complaint. It won't get you very far, but I can give you the forms." She went to a filing cabinet and pulled out a bunch of papers. "It's quadruplicate. Remember you keep the bottom copy," she snarled and dropped the papers on the desk.

I looked at them dumbly for a minute, got up, and left. As I went out the door, I heard her opening that file drawer. *How many times has she done that to somebody?* I considered going back and taking them, but for what?

Muriel wasn't interested in what was happening either. Her story had gotten good play. She'd even been on TV a couple of times. But I was old news and ready for wrapping fish.

I was in the crapper, but there were some good things. When I had gone by to thank Heinrich and ask about working, he'd paid me for that last Thursday night. Since Magda wasn't there, he even slipped me a roast beef sandwich. "This one's on me."

Mrs. Buthyre had been holding a letter for me. It was from Ephraim. He hadn't sent all the money, but some. "I'm on my own," he wrote. "My mother went off with a new guy right after I got here. She and Isaac moved to Salt Lake. I think he's a Mormon or something. Anyway, I got a job singing and cleaning up in a restaurant. They give me a place to sleep and meals so I don't have to spend much. And, by the way, I don't have to pay for drinks, which saves me a lot.

"They might give you a job, too. That is if you want one."

With the money from Heinrich and from Ephraim in my pocket, and the money I had left in my Cedar Rapids envelope, I was feeling I could handle things.

I took the two envelopes and headed for The Dew Drop. After all, I needed to head someplace.

And, damn, did I want a drink.

I walked in, and it was like nothing had changed. "Yous want a drink?" Sal greeted me.

Jonny hardly looked up as he lined up his next shot.

"Yeah, sure," I answered Sal.

"Yous got money?"

"Yeah, I got money." I put down a twenty.

"Look who's loaded," Chip commented. "You buyin' for the rest of us?"

I looked at him, at the others, at that drink. I picked up my change and put it in my pocket. "No, I don't…"

Picking up the shot glass of rye, I looked at it carefully, like I was studying something important. I handed it to Chip. "Here, you can have this one. Sorry it ain't tequila."

I walked to the door.

I want something, but it ain't really a drink.

"See you guys. See you around." On an impulse I headed for the bus station. But there was one more stop I had to make.

I hadn't bothered to go by The Shady Rest Home. Even if O'Rourke wanted me to come back to work, I knew it wasn't to be. But, before I left town, I wanted to see Morty, to say goodbye and wish him well.

The receptionist didn't recognize me. I explained that I'd worked nights, and she wanted to call O'Rourke and tell him I was there.

"That's not necessary," I explained. "There's this one pa … I mean resident I got to know. I wanted to stop by and say hello."

"The resident's name?"

"Morty Jones. He was in room twenty-two."

"Oh, yes. Let me call Mr. O'Rourke."

I sat in an uncomfortable chair covered with fake leather and made believe I was reading a *People* from months before.

O'Rourke walked up to me with his hand extended. "Cal," he said in a warm voice, "good to see you. I heard about your troubles. I want you to know—"

I interrupted him, "I'm leaving town. I just wanted to say goodbye to Morty Jones."

"You knew Morty?"

"Not really. He'd talk to me while I was cleaning his bathroom."

"Oh. That makes sense."

"What does?"

"Mr. Jones is no longer with us."

"He left?"

"Not exactly. He's dead."

"I'm sorry to hear that. He didn't seem that sick—not the last time I saw him."

"It wasn't his health. He committed suicide. Evidently he'd saved up his sleeping pills and took them all at once. Went to sleep—"

"I'm sorry."

"There was a letter. It was for you, but we didn't realize … It didn't really make sense." He held out a folded sheet of paper and watched as he unfolded it.

The note was short and to the point; written in block letters.

```
Calvin,
It's time for me to go home.
              Your friend, Morty
```

I sat in the park and reread Morty's letter. After the fifth read, I took out that silver lighter. The cops had given it back to me, and I'd been walking around with it not knowing if I should pawn it or just throw it in a dumpster. I set fire to the note, and when it was almost burned and I was feeling the flames, I dropped it into a garbage can. There was a brief flare and then nothing. I dropped the lighter into that can and walked away.

CHAPTER 26 - IN EVERY TOWN

There were three buses out of town that afternoon: to Dallas, to Saint Louis, and here. It wasn't a long trip. I sat next to this woman. She was heavy and unkempt. She was eating when I got on the bus—eating and dropping tuna salad on herself.

I wouldn't have sat next to her, but the only other vacant seat was next to a mother and her kid. She was staring at me. I know that stare; I've seen it many times—a combination of fear and disgust. So I sat where I was less unwelcome.

The woman, her name was Karen, wanted to talk. I didn't want to listen, but that didn't stop her. She was traveling from her home in Arkansas to live with her daughter. She was full of bubbly expectations that I knew were going to burst.

"I'll be a great help," she insisted; "I can help with the kids and the housekeeping. Haley Jean needs me. She really does. Otherwise, why I wouldn't have come. It isn't like I need her to take me in ..."

I could hear the lie in her voice and wondered if she believed it anyway.

About a hundred miles into the trip, Karen pulled out another sandwich. "Do you want half?"

I was hungry—kind of the way I felt a few hours after I had eaten some of Chan's chow mein, like there was something in my stomach, but it made me even hungrier. "What kind?" I asked even though I'd have taken anything.

"Ham and cheese."

"If you can spare it."

"Oh, I made a whole bag before I got on this bus. I'm running low now. Not much else to do on a bus. Eat and look out the window. At least with you I got somebody to talk at." She handed me half a sandwich and went back to talking. She talked and chewed at the same time, and pieces of white bread kept falling on her breasts. She'd pick them off, pop them into her mouth, and go right on.

I wasn't listening. Just chewing on that sandwich and wishing there was mustard and that I had something to drink.

Something to drink. Boy would I love a cold one. I pictured the guys back at The Dew Drop. *I bet there's a place just like it in the next town.* There has to be.

I imagined it. I imagined the people who'd be hanging out there, the kind who looked like they never went home, like they had no place to go.

Why did I leave? I had a life, friends. I could of found another place to live, work. O'Rourke would have been glad—

"Hey!" Karen's voice cut through my thoughts.

"What?"

"I asked ya a question."

"Sorry. I guess putting some food in my stomach—"

"Yeah, sure. So where are you from?"

"From?" I guess you could say ..." I stalled for time, not sure what I wanted to tell her.

"I guess you could say I'm from The Dew Drop Inne. There's one in every town."

"I don't get it."

"To be honest, neither do I."

We rode along. I rode in silence. I don't know if she was talking or not.

At the bus station I went to the phone booth, got the yellow pages and looked for bars. I was going to find another Dew Drop, another home. There was an ad, an Alcoholics Anonymous ad. I thought, why not, and came to this meeting instead. Tomorrow, maybe I'll see if there really is a Dew Drop in this town. For today, I'll share my story and drink bad coffee. For today, yeah for today, this might be home.

Author's Note

Tales From the Dew Drop Inne was not originally intended to be a novel. It started out as a single short story written for a new magazine, which was to be the creative voice for the Downtown Phoenix Writers' Meetup. This meetup group had become something of a writing home for me, so I went with a story that focused on the idea of creating a psychological family.

Then Salvatore Buttaci, a fellow author from the All Things That Matter Press community, asked me to write a short story for a contest he was organizing. Already comfortable with the characters of the Dew Drop, it was very easy to create another tale, this time a humorous account of sexual embarrassment, Angelica at the Dew Drop Inne.

With two connected stories under my belt and characters who were dying to express themselves, the rest of the book just seemed to flow.

A few advance readers have asked me why I set the novel in Albuquerque. The Dew Drop could be in any town. Indeed, my working subtitle had been "Because there's one in every town." I deliberately chose a city of which I had minimal knowledge and experience because there are such neighborhood bars everywhere, and in each of them there is a community of people desperately hanging on to a sense of belonging and family.

These are not successful people. Not the high and mighty, not even the middle of the pack, but also not those who have fallen off the ladder of life: these are the folks who hang on to the bottom rungs, but their lowly status doesn't mean that they lack values, comradeship, and meaning. Tales From the Dew Drop Inne tells their stories, and I hope in the process it reminds us all of the importance of each and every soul who tries to find worth in his or her life.

My own life is also filled with special characters. They have helped and nurtured this book's creation. Besides the members of that writers' meetup, I have to offer some specific thanks.

First and foremost is my wife Rosalyn. Roz listens when I read aloud, responds to questions with thought and humor, reads drafts and helps with my abysmal spelling and sometimes quirky grammar. She also takes photos when asked. I greatly appreciate her author's photo, taken at a local bar—Roscoe's on Seventh—the kind of place I almost never visit, but which was wonderfully consistent with my idea of The Dew Drop Inne.

Then there are the wonderful folks at All Things That Matter Press. Debbi Harris is an editor who provides support, love, and humor. The crew at ATTMP also put up with my gaffes and work with me in creating the best possible final product.

Before Debbi even sees the final draft, it is edited by my personal editor, Jacob Shaver. If there is one piece of advice I would offer to every would-be writer it is to find a Jake.

Finally, a word about the cover. Maggie Evans was kind enough to allow us to use this wonderful drawing. We had tried a number of other cover ideas when, acting on one of Roz's great suggestions, I searched the Internet for a piece of art. There was, a bar scene that spoke of companionship, stories, and an invitation to enter. I contacted Maggie, who, having checked out my writing, gave us the go ahead and searched for a usable computer file.

In the end, writing a book about a sense of family and belonging has also created a real life sense of family. Thanks, guys. Thank you all.
~ *Kenneth Weene*

About the Author

A New Englander by upbringing and inclination, Kenneth Weene is a teacher, psychologist and pastoral counselor by education. Having retired to Arizona, where he lives with his wife of forty-five years, Ken decided to fulfill a childhood passion and become a writer.

Ken's poetry and short stories have appeared in numerous publications - both print and electronic. *Tales From the Dew Drop Inne* is Ken's third novel, following *Memoirs From the Asylum* and *Widow's Walk*.

With two other novels and a novella waiting in the wings and a movie script currently under construction, Ken feels more creative now then he has ever been.